BEST 倍斯特出版事業有限公司
Best Publishing Ltd.

U0066415

一次就考到

# 雅思聽力

## 準確定位關鍵訊息且能靈活應答

Amanda Chou
◎ 著

7+

MP3

**三大學習特色** 強化「填空題」拼字能力／提升聽力「專注力」和答題「穩定度」／掌握生活場景和學術場景循環必考字彙

**靈活應對雅思聽力出題：**收錄超過1000題填空題，強化考生對聆聽數字的反應力及拼寫出所有生活場景字彙，即刻達到應試填空題**答對率100%**。。

**補強聽力專注力和答題穩定度：**藉由「影子跟讀法」修正聽力專注力，提升聽section 3和4長段落訊息時的定位能力和答題穩定度。

**豐富各類別語句表達：**藉由書中各式文章，累積各種語句轉換和表達，同義轉換能力猛飆升，無懼複選題和其他題型變化的出題。

# 序 Preface

　　劍橋雅思 14 於近期問世了，也代表著考生在備考時，有多四回的聽力模擬試題供於練習和衝刺用，考生更關心的應該是命題的趨勢和變化，因為越是新出的劍橋題本越是反映出命題的變化，越舊的題本則鋒芒已老，在備考上較不具參考價值了。劍橋雅思 14 在填空題的命題上還是跟劍橋雅思 13 很類似，除了第四回測驗的 section 4 部分是選擇題，其他都是填空題，也就是每回測驗的 40 題題目中，有近 20 題甚至 30 題都是填空題。填空題代表著必須要準確聽到該字並拼寫正確才答對，所以考生必須要強化的是生活類場景的拼字能力，例如：數字、日期、月份和常考生活字等等。

　　以四回測驗中各個第一個部分（Section 1）的命題來做比較：

- **Test 1** Section 1 Crime Report Form 為例，包含了國籍、常考生活字彙（例如：furniture, Park, museum等字）、數字、較長的一段數字（crime reference number）、日期＋月份和顏色。
- **Test 2** Section 1 Total Health Clinic 中，包含了較長的一段數字（phone number）、日期＋月份、地名拼寫和常考生活字彙（例如：manager, knee, tennis, shoulder和vitamins等）。

- **Test 3** Section 1 Flanders Conference Hotel 中，包含了兩組數字、公司名和常考生活字彙（例如：pool, airport, sea 等等）。
- Test 4 Section 1 Enquiry about Booking Hotel Room for Event 中，則包含了數字和常考生活字彙例如：roses, trees, stage, speech和support等）。

　　關於四回測驗中各個第四部份（Section 4）的命題則可以清楚知道是常考的生活字彙（單字難度在 4000 單以內），本書秉持以官方試題命題聽力測驗會挖空的常考生活字彙作為基礎，規劃了三個部分：短對話、短段落和長段落，包含這些基礎生活字彙的題材和填空練習，書中還有海量的填空題練習**超過 1000 題**提供考生充分練習（每本劍橋雅思的填空題總數約 80 題），並以影子跟讀的設計來強化聽力專注力。此外，除了基礎常考字的練習外，再以這些基礎作延伸，涵蓋許多更高階的字彙，這些在聽力測驗學術演講題材以及閱讀測驗中都會常出現。密集演練這些填空題，有效縮短考生在應考中填寫答案的時間，立刻正確拼寫出該字詞，不會浪費數秒在閱讀或於聽力測驗中思考時，邊寫邊回到定位的段落去找該高階名詞。

# 序 Preface

關於 section 2 和 section 3 的選擇題和配對題，書中的題材跟許多語彙表達，提供考生參考作答方式以及方向，考生則需要多注意同義轉換。另外對於不習慣聽 section 3 和 section 4 答題的考生（已經能掌握 section 1 和 section 2 聽力出題模式），可以充分使用書中「短對話」和「長對話」練習，提升答題穩定性和正確性，聽力測驗答完後有時間稍靜下心來等待發閱讀試題。

寫官方試題僅在演練跟熟悉試題，大部分的考生不太容易在剛寫完的所有聽力試題（例如：劍橋雅思 9-14）後就能應考（每回聽力測驗僅需花 40 分鐘，每本劍橋雅思有四回測驗，所以兩個小時 40 分鐘可以寫完一本，數天內就完成備考），而官方試題提供的練習不多，可用於考前兩周的衝刺。其實聽力測驗還包含很多面向，一個人的聽力專注力、聽力理解力，是需要長期養成的。本書中的練習內容涵蓋量極廣，提供考生練習，幫助考生在短期間內突破。透過這些海量的練習，考生若都能聽對每題填空題的答案並且拼寫正確，相信不論在寫哪回官方試題，對答案時都會信心滿滿，有把握達到 7-7.5 以上的成績。

最後要推薦的是《一次就考到雅思聽力6.5+》，與本書為姊妹篇，這兩本都適用於各校的大一和大二英文課程，老師可以參考這兩本書用於平日課堂測驗讓學生練習聽力，省下思考出試題的時間。裡面也包含了海量的聽力試題，寫完這兩本等同於要報考大學指定科目考試國文，但已經唸完兩本古文觀止了，想要不拿高分都難呀！祝各位考生獲取理想成績。

# 收到的貨物與出貨單內容不符－訂單編號＋日期＋月份

▶▶ 影子跟讀「短對話」練習 🎧 MP3 022

此篇為「**影子跟讀短對話練習**」，規劃了由聽「**短對話**」的 shadowing 練習，從最基礎、最易上手的部分切入雅思聽力備考，熟悉各生活場景類的用字，現在就一起動身，開始聽「**短對話**」！

Michelle: Thanks for the shipment, but I think there is a problem. This is not the right order for us.

蜜雪兒：謝謝你的出貨，可是這批貨有點問題，這跟我們訂的貨不一樣。

Justin: Right, can you explain further, please?

賈斯丁：是嗎？可以說清楚一點嗎？

Michelle: Sure, do you have a copy of the packing list handy?

蜜雪兒：當然，你手邊有我們的出貨單嗎？

Justin: Just a minute, I will look it up. Here it is.

賈斯丁：稍等，我找一下，找到了。

Michelle: On the packing list it shows that we ordered a complete filter system which is housing plus a filter pad, but what we received is only a filter pad replacement. Can you please check your record and send us the filter housing ASAP please?

蜜雪兒：在出貨單上顯示我們訂的是整組的過濾器，就是過濾器再加上濾網，可是實際上貨物裡面只有濾網。你可以查一下你的出貨紀錄然後趕快補一個過濾器給我們嗎？

Justin: Ok, I will check with my coworker and let you know shortly.

賈斯丁：好的，我跟我的同事求證一下再跟你說。

# 一本就搞定，所有考生均適用

- 規劃適合所有考生的學習模式，基礎型考生也能簡單自學上手，從「**短對話**」開始練習**影子跟讀**和**填空練習**。考生也能彈性使用本書，按照自己程度選擇特定的篇章練習。

- 短對話練習上手後，進階至「**短段落**」和「**長段落**」練習，都練習完即刻具備寫一整回官方試題的能力。

- **一本就搞定**，節省翻閱數本官方題本練習，書籍中更以**中英對照**呈現全然貼近考生學習需求。

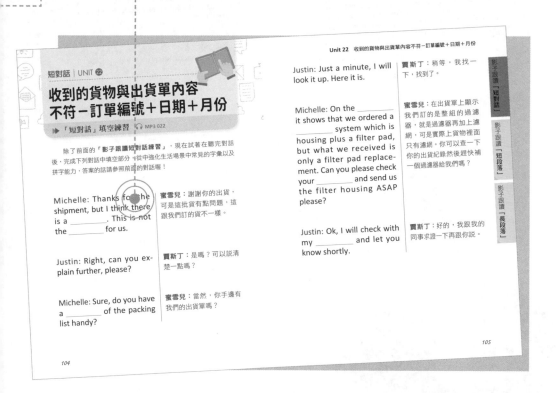

短對話 | UNIT 22

## 收到的貨物與出貨單內容不符－訂單編號＋日期＋月份

▶▶「短對話」填空練習　🎧 MP3 022

除了前面的「**影子跟讀短對話練習**」，現在試著在聽完對話後，完成下列對話中填空部分，從中強化生活場景中常見的字彙以及拼字能力，答案的話請參照前面的對話喔！

Michelle: Thanks for the shipment, but I think there is a _____. This is not the _____ for us.

蜜雪兒：謝謝你的出貨，可是這批貨有點問題，這跟我們訂的貨不一樣。

Justin: Right, can you explain further, please?

賈斯丁：是嗎？可以說清楚一點嗎？

Michelle: Sure, do you have a _____ of the packing list handy?

蜜雪兒：當然，你手邊有我們的出貨單嗎？

### Unit 22　收到的貨物與出貨單內容不符－訂單編號＋日期＋月份

Justin: Just a minute, I will look it up. Here it is.

賈斯丁：稍等，我找一下，找到了。

Michelle: On the _____ it shows that we ordered a _____ system which is housing plus a filter pad, but what we received is only a filter pad replacement. Can you please check your _____ and send us the filter housing ASAP please?

蜜雪兒：在出貨單上顯示我們訂的是整組的過濾器，就是過濾器再加上濾網，可是實際上貨物裡面只有濾網。你可以查一下你的出貨紀錄然後趕快補一個過濾器給我們嗎？

Justin: Ok, I will check with my _____ and let you know shortly.

賈斯丁：好的，我跟我的同事求證一下再跟你說。

影子跟讀「短對話」
影子跟讀「短段落」
影子跟讀「長段落」

104

105

# Instructions
## 使用說明

# Batman 蝙蝠俠 ❶ — 內科醫生＋常考名詞和形容詞

▶ 影子跟讀「短段落」練習 🎧 MP3 042

此篇為「影子跟讀短段落練習」，規劃了由聽「短段落」的 shadowing 練習，強化考生定位和聆聽數個句子的專注力，聽 section 3 和 section 4 都覺得瞬間變得簡單，現在就一起動身，開始聽「短段落」！

Bruce Wayne was born into a wealthy family in Gotham City. When he was a kid, he witnessed his parents, the physician Dr.Thomas Wayne and his wife Martha Wayne, getting murdered by a mugger with a gun in front of his very eyes. He was traumatized but swore revenge in all criminals. Growing up, he became a successful business magnate. He was an American billionaire and owned the Wayne Enterprises. In his everyday identity, he acted like a playboy, a heavy drinker, just like many other wealthy men.

布魯斯・韋恩出生在高譚市一個富裕的家庭。當他還是個孩子時，他眼睜睜的看著他的父母，托馬斯・韋恩博士和他的妻子瑪莎・韋恩，被一個搶劫犯槍殺身亡。他受到創傷，但誓言對罪

182

犯復仇。長大後，他成為了一個成功的商業鉅子。他是美國的一個億萬富翁，並擁有韋恩企業。他日常的身份，就像一個花花公子，天天喝酒，就與許多其他有錢的男人一樣。

But in reality, he did his best maintaining his physical fitness and mental acuity. He also developed a bat inspired persona to fight crime. Dressing up as Batman, Wayne kept the city safe and fought against crimes for most of his night life.

但在現實中，他保持最好的體能和敏銳的智能。他也開發了一個由蝙蝠作為啟發的人物來打擊犯罪。裝扮成蝙蝠俠，韋恩在他大部分的夜生活時保持城市的安全及打擊犯罪。

Batman does not possess any superpowers. He relies on his genius intellect, physical prowess, martial arts abilities, detective skills, science and technology, vast wealth, and an indomitable will. Even Superman considers Batman to be one of the most brilliant human beings on the planet.

蝙蝠俠沒有任何超能力。他依靠他天生的智慧、高強的體能、精湛的武藝、偵探的技能、科學與技術、巨大的財富和不屈不撓的意志。即便是超人都認為蝙蝠俠是這個星球上最聰明的人類之一。

183

## ⟶ 影子跟讀「短段落」練習　🎧 MP3 042

此部分為「影子跟讀短段落練習❷」，請重新播放音檔並完成試題。現在就一起動身，開始完成「短段落練習❷」吧！

Bruce Wayne was born into a 1.＿＿＿＿＿ in Gotham City. When he was a 2.＿＿＿＿＿, he witnessed his parents, the 3.＿＿＿＿＿ Dr. Thomas Wayne and his wife Martha Wayne, getting murdered by a 4.＿＿＿＿＿ with a gun in front of his very eyes. He was traumatized but swore 5.＿＿＿＿＿ in all criminals. Growing up, he became a successful 6.＿＿＿＿＿. He was an American 7.＿＿＿＿＿ and owned the Wayne Enterprises. In his everyday 8.＿＿＿＿＿, he acted like a 9.＿＿＿＿＿, a heavy drinker, just like many other wealthy men.

But in reality, he did his best maintaining his 10.＿＿＿＿＿ and mental 11.＿＿＿＿＿. He also developed a bat inspired 12.＿＿＿＿＿ to fight crime. Batman does not possess any superpowers. He relies on his 13.＿＿＿＿＿ intellect, physical prowess, martial arts abilities, 14.＿＿＿＿＿ skills, science and technology, vast wealth, and an 15.＿＿＿＿＿. Even Superman considers Batman to be one of the most 16.＿＿＿＿＿ human beings on the planet.

## ⟶ 參考答案

1. wealthy family
2. kid
3. physician
4. mugger
5. revenge
6. business magnate
7. billionaire
8. identity
9. playboy
10. physical fitness
11. acuity
12. persona
13. genius
14. detective
15. indomitable will
16. brilliant

## 真題重現+海量練習

- 所有出題均根據官方聽力和閱讀中常見的常考字（**真題重現**），篩選掉「過難」跟「不常考」的字彙，在考場上，腦海中更會浮現似曾相識的感覺，應試時更無往不利。
- 包含超過 **1000 題**以上的填空練習，為單本官方試題近 **12.5 倍**的練習量，實力絕對倍數成長，一次性獲取高分。

*Instructions*
使用說明

# 心理學：咖啡和複利效應－數字＋常見名詞＋商學專業字 ❷

▶影子跟讀「實戰練習」 🎧 MP3 062

此篇為「影子跟讀實戰練習」，規劃了由聽「實際考試長度的英文內容」的 shadowing 練習，經由先前的兩個部份的練習，已能逐步掌握聽一定句數的英文內容，現在經由實際考試長度的聽力內容來練習，讓耳朵適應聽這樣長度的英文內容，提升在考場時的答題**穩定度和適應性**，進而獲取理想成績，現在就一起動身，開始由聽「**實戰練習**」！（如果聽這部份且跟讀練習的難度還是太高請重複前兩個部份的練習數次後再做這部分的練習喔！）

A cup of coffee from big brands? Hmm... so tempting. Sorry for setting a bad example myself, but it's actually a good start for today's topic "the compound effect." What does a cup of coffee have to do with this? Every day whether you are on your way to the office, or whether you are feeling exhausted after a long day at school, it's so tempting to have a cup of coffee, sitting in a comfy chair and a room with a perfect lighting. All of a sudden, fatigue and other things are overridden...like it's just a cup of coffee or it's just NT150 dollars.

一杯來自咖啡大廠的咖啡…嗯…如此吸引人…抱歉自己做了

很不好的示範，但是實際上卻是今天主題「累加效應」很好的開端。一杯咖啡與這個有甚麼關聯性呢？每天不論你是前往上班途中或是你在學校漫長的一天後身感疲憊，有杯咖啡是如此吸引人，坐在舒適的椅子和有著恰如其分的燈光下。突然間，疲累和其他事情都被蓋過了…像是只是一杯咖啡或者是僅花費 150 元新台幣。

Although we have been warned or urged not to spend money buying a coffee, we just cannot help buying it whenever we feel there is a need for us to lighten up our mood or something. We have put behind what many experts have said or mentioned in those articles. But little things do matter. Doing a basic calculation yourself, you can surely find how significant that is. Accumulated fees can somehow astound most of us.

雖然我們已受到警告或規勸不要將金錢花費在購買咖啡，但是每當我們覺得有需要能讓我們打起精神或什麼的，我們又無法克制地買了它。我們將許多專家所說的話或在那些文章中提到的部分都拋諸到腦後。但是這一丁點的小事卻至關重要。自己做一個基本計算，你可以確定發現影響會是多麼重大。累積的費用令我們大多數的人感到吃驚。

Let me do a basic calculation for you. A white-collar office lady who buys another brand's coffee, whose price is significantly lower than that of the big brand's. Say 55 NT dollars for a latte. She buys a cup of coffee per day.

## 極限突破、準確定位

- 習慣聽「**長段落**」訊息，有效協助定位section 3和section 4出題點，提升**答題穩定度**和**應試能力**，不分神且耐心聽，訊息考點就會出現（慌亂很容易造成這部分答題的失分）。
- 藉由填空測驗，強化應試時的**拼字能力**，並一次就將正確的答案填寫在答案欄上。

---

### ▶▶ 影子跟讀「實戰練習」　🎧 MP3 062

此部分為「**影子跟讀實戰練習 2**」，請重新播放音檔並完成試題，除了能提升並修正拼寫能力外，也可以藉由音檔注意自己專注力和定位聽力訊息部份，走神或定位錯都會影響在實際考場中的表現，尤其在 section 3 和 4 影響的得分會更明顯，現在就一起動身，開始完成「**實戰練習 2**」吧！

Sorry for setting a bad example myself, but it's actually a good start for today's topic "the 1._____". Everyday whether you are on your way to the 2._____, or whether you are feeling exhausted after a long day at school, it's so tempting to have a cup of coffee, sitting in a 3._____ and a room with a perfect lighting. All of a sudden, 4._____ and other things are overridden... like it's just a cup of coffee or it's just NT5._____

We have put behind what many 6._____ have said or mentioned in those articles. But little things do matter. Doing a basic 7._____ yourself, you can surely find how significant that is. Accumulated 8._____ can somehow astound most of us.

A white-collar 9._____ who buys another brand's coffee, whose price is significantly lower than that of the big brand's. Say 55 NT dollars for a 10._____. She buys a cup of coffee per day. There are 11._____

298

____ in a year. She buys 5 cups of coffee per week. We multiply that by 52, and the result is NT 12._____ per year.

No wonder, an expert once said, if you're earning a 13._____ right after you graduate, then you probably shouldn't be drinking coffee of huge brands, and it's the accumulated fee of other brands...

Sometimes people just don't think it's a big deal or something. That's why people have a hard time looking at what's in their 14._____ at the end of the month. According to the fee calculation, you can buy an 15._____, if you quit drinking coffee for two years.

We are looking at NT 16._____ which is close to two months' income for a new grad. It's scary. We are responsible for every choice we make. Every day we tend to ignore little things. Some of my 17._____ even have 18._____, but they are not making smart choices.

Being willing to change is always a great start in life. For example, before starting a 19._____ of my own, I used to buy unnecessary things, thinking that 20._____ is easily earned. Now I don't want to drink coffee any more. Instead I drink water. Another thing which also relates to today's topic "the compound effect" is the calorie. You're

299

*Instructions*
使用說明

# CONTENTS 目次

## Part 2　影子跟讀「短段落」

## Part 3 影子跟讀－「長段落」

# 房屋修繕－月份＋星期＋數字

▶▶ 影子跟讀「短對話」練習 🎧 MP3 001

　　此篇為**「影子跟讀短對話練習」**，規劃了由聽**「短對話」**的 shadowing 練習，從最基礎、最易上手的部分切入雅思聽力備考，熟悉各生活場景類的用字，現在就一起動身，開始聽**「短對話」**！

Peter: Hello Mrs. Moore. I came to see you today because I reported the problem of the leaking tap in my bathroom last month, and you promised me the plumber would be here in a few days, but till now he is nowhere to be seen still.

彼得：摩爾太太您好，我今天來是因為我上個月就跟你說過浴室的水龍頭在漏水。你答應我水電工這幾天就會來，可是一直都沒有人來修。

Mrs. Moore: Oh... my apology. I will get onto it on Monday.

摩爾太太：不好意思，我星期一會馬上辦。

Peter: Do you realize how much we have to pay for our last water bill? It cost an extra 50 dollars! I am only a student, and I don't make a lot of money and I hope you are willing to cover the extra cost until the tap is fixed. If the plumber does not rock up on Monday, I will hire one to fix it myself and send the bill to you.

彼得：你知道我們上個月的水費繳多少錢嗎？比平常多 50 美金。我只是個學生，賺的錢不多，我希望在水龍頭修好之前你要負擔額外的水費。如果水電工星期一再不來修，我只好自己請人來修然後把帳單寄給你。

影子跟讀「短對話」

影子跟讀「短段落」

影子跟讀「長段落」

# 房屋修繕－月份＋星期＋數字

▶▶ 「短對話」填空練習　🎧 MP3 001

　　除了前面的**「影子跟讀短對話練習」**，現在試著在聽完對話後，完成下列對話中填空部分，從中強化生活場景中常見的字彙以及拼字能力，答案的話請參照前面的對話喔！

Peter: Hello Mrs. Moore. I came to see you today because I reported the problem of the _____ tap in my _____ last _____ __ , and you promised me the _____ would be here in a few days, but till now he is nowhere to be seen still.

彼得：摩爾太太您好，我今天來是因為我上個月就跟你說過浴室的水龍頭在漏水。你答應我水電工這幾天就會來，可是一直都沒有人來修。

Mrs. Moore: Oh... my _____. I will get onto it on _____.

摩爾太太：不好意思，我星期一會馬上辦。

Peter: Do you realize how much we have to pay for our last _____? It cost an extra _____! I am only a _____, and I don't make a lot of _____ and I hope you are willing to cover the _____ until the tap is fixed. If the _____ does not rock up on _____, I will hire one to fix it myself and send _____ to you.

彼得：你知道我們上個月的水費繳多少錢嗎？比平常多 50 美金。我只是個學生，賺的錢不多，我希望在水龍頭修好之前你要負擔額外的水費。如果水電工星期一再不來修，我只好自己請人來修然後把帳單寄給你。

影子跟讀「短對話」

影子跟讀「短段落」

影子跟讀「長段落」

# 退租押金－家俱＋數字＋議價

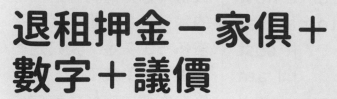

▶▶ 影子跟讀「短對話」練習 🎧 MP3 002

此篇為「影子跟讀短對話練習」，規劃了由聽「短對話」的 shadowing 練習，從最基礎、最易上手的部分切入雅思聽力備考，熟悉各生活場景類的用字，現在就一起動身，開始聽「短對話」！

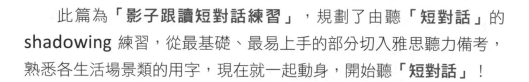

Mr. Ferguson: I am happy with the general condition of the wall and the carpet, but the kitchen cabinet doors need to be replaced. The condition is appalling. I will have to deduct USD 150 from your bond.

佛格森先生：這房子的牆面及地毯大概的情況都還好，可是廚房儲物櫃的門需要更換，怎麼會弄得這麼糟？我必須扣你 150 美金的押金。

Claire: I do apologize, my boyfriend thought the door was jammed and he pulled it too hard. The hinges just

克萊兒：真的很抱歉，我男朋友以為櫥櫃門卡住了就用力拉，誰知道太用力了，櫃子的樞軸就掉下來

came off. I think you can easily repair it if you get a handyman in. It would not cost USD 150, would it? I think USD 100 would be a fair price. I mean the condition of the cabinet door was not too flash when we moved in to start with. You can see for yourself we do try to take a good care of this place.

了。我覺得如果找個雜工來處理應該很容易更換，這應該不需要 150 美金吧！100 應該就可以了吧！因為我們搬進來的時候櫥櫃門本來就有點舊，你應該也看的出來我們一直都很照顧這個房子。

影子跟讀「短對話」

影子跟讀「短段落」

影子跟讀「長段落」

# 退租押金－家俱＋數字＋議價

▶▶ 「短對話」填空練習 🎧 MP3 002

　　除了前面的「**影子跟讀短對話練習**」，現在試著在聽完對話後，完成下列對話中填空部分，從中強化生活場景中常見的字彙以及拼字能力，答案的話請參照前面的對話喔！

Mr. Ferguson: I am happy with the general _____ of the _____ and the _____, but the _____ cabinet _____ need to be replaced. The _____ is appalling. I will have to deduct USD _____ from your _____.

佛格森先生：這房子的牆面及地毯大概的情況都還好，可是廚房儲物櫃的門需要更換，怎麼會弄得這麼糟？我必須扣你 150 美金的押金。

Claire: I do _____, my _____ thought the _____ was jammed and he pulled it too hard. The _____

克萊兒：真的很抱歉，我男朋友以為櫥櫃門卡住了就用力拉，誰知道太用力了，櫃子的樞軸就掉下來

_____ just came off. I think you can easily _____ it if you get a _____ in. It would not cost USD _____ ___, would it? I think USD _____ would be a fair price. I mean the condition of the _____ was not too flash when we moved in to start with. You can see for yourself we do try to take a good care of this place.

了。我覺得如果找個雜工來處理應該很容易更換，這應該不需要 150 美金吧！100 應該就可以了吧！因為我們搬進來的時候櫥櫃門本來就有點舊，你應該也看的出來我們一直都很照顧這個房子。

影子跟讀「短對話」

影子跟讀「短段落」

影子跟讀「長段落」

# 電話安裝紛爭－帳單 ＋安裝費＋客服

▶▶ 影子跟讀「短對話」練習 　🎧 MP3 003

　　此篇為「**影子跟讀短對話練習**」，規劃了由聽「**短對話**」的 shadowing 練習，從最基礎、最易上手的部分切入雅思聽力備考，熟悉各生活場景類的用字，現在就一起動身，開始聽「**短對話**」！

| | |
|---|---|
| Mark: How is your home phone going? | 馬克：你的家用電話都裝好了嗎？ |
| Andy: It is going ok, but I received the bill asking for installation fee, and I remembered clearly there is no installation fee. | 安迪：還好，可是我收到一張帳單說要收安裝費，我記得很清楚你說過沒有安裝費的。 |
| Mark: There is no installation fee, if you are switching from other phone company, but for the new client | 馬克：如果你有安裝過別家公司的電話，那是沒有安裝費的。可是如果是全新用戶那就會有。 |

there is an installation charge.

Andy: Well, that is not what I was told. I would not have signed up if I knew, there is going to be installation charge. What form do I have to sign to cancel the service?

安迪：可是我聽到的不是這樣，我如果知道有安裝費用我就不會選擇你們公司。那我要取消，要填什麼表格呢？

Mark: I am sorry you are under the wrong impression, let me check with my boss and see what I can do.

馬克：不好意思你可能誤會我的意思，讓我問一下我的上司看能怎麼處理。

Andy: Now you are talking, I am sure you don't want to lose a customer.

安迪：這才對，你一定也不想失去一個客戶。

# 電話安裝紛爭－帳單＋安裝費＋客服

▶▶ 「短對話」填空練習 🎧 MP3 003

除了前面的「影子跟讀短對話練習」，現在試著在聽完對話後，完成下列對話中填空部分，從中強化生活場景中常見的字彙以及拼字能力，答案的話請參照前面的對話喔！

| | |
|---|---|
| Mark: How is your _____ _ going? | 馬克：你的家用電話都裝好了嗎？ |
| Andy: It is going ok, but I received _____ asking for _____, and I re-membered clearly there is no _____. | 安迪：還好，可是我收到一張帳單說要收安裝費，我記得很清楚你說過沒有安裝費的。 |
| Mark: There is no _____ _, if you are switching from other phone _____ _, but for the new _____ | 馬克：如果你有安裝過別家公司的電話，那是沒有安裝費的。可是如果是全新用戶那就會有。 |

__ there is an installation __
_____.

Andy: Well, that is not what I was told. I would not have signed up if I knew, there is going to be installation charge. What __ _____ do I have to sign to _____ the _____?

安迪：可是我聽到的不是這樣，我如果知道有安裝費用我就不會選擇你們公司。那我要取消，要填什麼表格呢？

Mark: I am sorry you are under the wrong _____ __, let me check with my __ _____ and see what I can do.

馬克：不好意思你可能誤會我的意思，讓我問一下我的上司看能怎麼處理。

Andy: Now you are talking, I am sure you don't want to lose a _____.

安迪：這才對，你一定也不想失去一個客戶。

影子跟讀「短對話」

影子跟讀「短段落」

影子跟讀「長段落」

# 報價同等品－詢價＋機台＋客戶溝通

▶▶ 影子跟讀「短對話」練習 🎧 MP3 004

　　此篇為**「影子跟讀短對話練習」**，規劃了由聽**「短對話」**的 shadowing 練習，從最基礎、最易上手的部分切入雅思聽力備考，熟悉各生活場景類的用字，現在就一起動身，開始聽**「短對話」**！

Linda: Hey Jamie, I have bad news for you, the part that you enquired yesterday is discontinued, and they do have a replacement, but the maker would need your machine type and serial number to determine whether the new part would suit your machine.

琳達：嗨！傑米，我有個壞的消息要跟你説，你昨天詢價的那個組件已經停產了，原廠是有替代品，可是你需要提供機台號碼還有型號製造商才能確認替代品能不能用在你的機台上。

Jamie: Right, thanks for letting me know, but I don't

傑米：好的，謝謝你跟我説，我手邊目前沒有這些

have the information handy. I need to check with the end user and ask them to provide the information. I might have to get back to you on Monday or even on Tuesday.

資訊，我需要跟客戶確認。可能要下星期一或甚至到星期二才能回覆給你。

Linda: No pressure! Just call me back whenever you got the detail.

琳達：沒問題，有資料再打給我就好。

影子跟讀「短對話」

影子跟讀「短段落」

影子跟讀「長段落」

# 報價同等品－詢價＋機台＋客戶溝通

▶▶ 「短對話」填空練習 🎧 MP3 004

　　除了前面的「**影子跟讀短對話練習**」，現在試著在聽完對話後，完成下列對話中填空部分，從中強化生活場景中常見的字彙以及拼字能力，答案的話請參照前面的對話喔！

Linda: Hey Jamie, I have bad news for you, the part that you enquired _____ is _____, and they do have a _____, but the maker would need your _____ type and _____ to determine whether the _____ would suit your _____.

琳達：嗨！傑米，我有個壞的消息要跟你説，你昨天詢價的那個組件已經停產了，原廠是有替代品，可是你需要提供機台號碼還有型號製造商才能確認替代品能不能用在你的機台上。

Jamie: Right, thanks for letting me know, but I don't have the _____. I need

傑米：好的，謝謝你跟我説，我手邊目前沒有這些資訊，我需要跟客戶確

to check with the _____ __ and ask them to provide the _____. I might have to get back to you on ____ _____ or even on _____ __.

認。可能要下星期一或甚至到星期二才能回覆給你。

Linda: No _____! Just call me back whenever you got the _____.

**琳達：**沒問題，有資料再打給我就好。

*33*

# 規格不清楚－詢價單＋型號（數字＋英文字）

▶▶ 影子跟讀「短對話」練習　🎧 MP3 005

此篇為**「影子跟讀短對話練習」**，規劃了由聽**「短對話」**的 shadowing 練習，從最基礎、最易上手的部分切入雅思聽力備考，熟悉各生活場景類的用字，現在就一起動身，開始聽**「短對話」**！

| | |
|---|---|
| Tom: Hi Rosie, thanks for the enquiry, but it seems a bit confusing. Can I just go through the details with you please? | 湯姆：蘿西您好，謝謝你的詢價單，可是明細有點不清楚，我想跟你再確認一下好嗎？ |
| Rosie: Of course, what seems to be the problem? | 蘿西：沒問題，是哪裡不清楚呢？ |
| Tom: The part number that you provided doesn't seem | 湯姆：你提供的型號不太像我們公司的標準型號， |

like our standard part number and I double checked the database, it is not our part.

我也重新確認過公司的系統，我們沒有這個型號。

Rosie: Right, can you tell me what your standard part number looks like?

蘿西：這樣啊，那你可以跟我說你們公司的型號大概是怎麼樣？

Tom: Sure, for pumps, it normally started with PS34. The number you provided is KS8A, I think it could have been PS34, but you'd better check again with the end user just to be on the safe side.

湯姆：可以，如果是幫浦的話，通常是 PS34 開頭的，你給我的型號是 KS8A，我猜有可能是 PS34，可是你最好跟客戶再確認一下。

# 規格不清楚－詢價單＋型號（數字＋英文字）

▶▶「短對話」填空練習 🎧 MP3 005

　　除了前面的**「影子跟讀短對話練習」**，現在試著在聽完對話後，完成下列對話中填空部分，從中強化生活場景中常見的字彙以及拼字能力，答案的話請參照前面的對話喔！

---

Tom: Hi Rosie, thanks for the ＿＿＿＿＿, but it seems a bit ＿＿＿＿＿. Can I just go through the ＿＿＿＿＿ with you please?

湯姆：蘿西您好，謝謝你的詢價單，可是明細有點不清楚，我想跟你再確認一下好嗎？

Rosie: Of course, what seems to be the ＿＿＿＿＿?

蘿西：沒問題，是哪裡不清楚呢？

Tom: The part number that you provided doesn't seem like our ＿＿＿＿＿ part

湯姆：你提供的型號不太像我們公司的標準型號，我也重新確認過公司的系

number and I double checked the _____, it is not our part.

統，我們沒有這個型號。

Rosie: Right, can you tell me what your _____ part number looks like?

蘿西：這樣啊，那你可以跟我說你們公司的型號大概是怎麼樣？

Tom: Sure, for _____, it _____ started with _____. The number you provided is _____, I think it could have been _____, but you'd better check again with the end user just to be on the _____ side.

湯姆：可以，如果是幫浦的話，通常是 PS34 開頭的，你給我的型號是 KS8A，我猜有可能是 PS34，可是你最好跟客戶再確認一下。

影子跟讀「短對話」

影子跟讀「短段落」

影子跟讀「長段落」

# 修改規格請重報－
# 詢價單＋設備＋客戶溝通

▶▶ 影子跟讀「短對話」練習 🎧 MP3 006

　　此篇為**「影子跟讀短對話練習」**，規劃了由聽**「短對話」**的 shadowing 練習，從最基礎、最易上手的部分切入雅思聽力備考，熟悉各生活場景類的用字，現在就一起動身，開始聽**「短對話」**！

| | |
|---|---|
| Gina: Hello, Kevin. How's going? You know the enquiry I sent you the other day for two knife rollers? | 吉娜：凱文您好，你記得我前幾天傳給你的詢價單嗎？就是詢價兩個滾刀那張。 |
| Kevin: Yes, I can recall. | 凱文：有，我記得。 |
| Gina: I just got off the phone with the client, and they are thinking about replacing the complete cut- | 吉娜：客戶剛打來說他們想乾脆把整組的裁切設備更新，升級成最新型的自動系統。你可以幫我報價 |

ting unit and upgrading it to the new automatic system. Is it possible for you to send us another quotation for a completed cutting unit with one spare roller please? Don't worry about these two rollers.

一組新的裁切設備加上一個備品滾刀？這兩組滾刀就不用報了。

Kevin: Ok, but I have to check whether the new cutting unit can be installed onto your client's machine first. I know some of them are not compatible with the original machine.

凱文：我知道了，可是我要先查一下新的裁切設備是不是可以裝在你們客戶的機台上，因為有些舊的機型沒有辦法修改。

影子跟讀「短對話」

影子跟讀「短段落」

影子跟讀「長段落」

# 修改規格請重報－詢價單＋設備＋客戶溝通

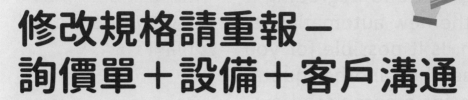

▶▶ 「短對話」填空練習 🎧 MP3 006

除了前面的**「影子跟讀短對話練習」**，現在試著在聽完對話後，完成下列對話中填空部分，從中強化生活場景中常見的字彙以及拼字能力，答案的話請參照前面的對話喔！

Gina: Hello, Kevin. How's going? You know the _____ _____ I sent you the other day for _____?

吉娜：凱文您好，你記得我前幾天傳給你的詢價單嗎？就是詢價兩個滾刀那張。

Kevin: Yes, I can recall.

凱文：有，我記得。

Gina: I just got off the _____ _____ with the _____, and they are thinking about replacing the complete cutting unit and _____ it to the new _____. Is it

吉娜：客戶剛打來說他們想乾脆把整組的裁切設備更新，升級成最新型的自動系統。你可以幫我報價一組新的裁切設備加上一個備品滾刀？這兩組滾刀

40

possible for you to send us another _____ for a completed cutting unit with one _____ please? Don't worry about these __ _____.

就不用報了。

Kevin: Ok, but I have to check whether the new cutting unit can be _____ __ onto your client's _____ first. I know some of them are not _____ with the _____.

凱文：我知道了，可是我要先查一下新的裁切設備是不是可以裝在你們客戶的機台上，因為有些舊的機型沒有辦法修改。

影子跟讀「短對話」

影子跟讀「短段落」

影子跟讀「長段落」

# 交期太長向廠商詢問原因－報價單＋星期＋客戶溝通

▶▶ 影子跟讀「短對話」練習　🎧 MP3 007

此篇為「**影子跟讀短對話練習**」，規劃了由聽「**短對話**」的 shadowing 練習，從最基礎、最易上手的部分切入雅思聽力備考，熟悉各生活場景類的用字，現在就一起動身，開始聽「**短對話**」！

---

Michael: Hi Zoe, thanks for your quotation. I did notice something unusual, and I thought I'd better check with you again.

麥可：柔伊你好，謝謝你的報價，報價單有點不尋常，我想我最好再跟你確認一次。

Zoe: Of course. You are referring to the quotation I sent yesterday if I am not wrong?

柔伊：當然，如果我沒想錯的話，你是指我昨天傳的那張嗎？

Michael: Yeah, that's it.

麥可：是的，沒錯。

Zoe: Oh..., what is wrong with it?

柔伊：噢…是哪裡有問題呢？

Michael: You know we ordered the same thing last year, but the delivery was only 4 weeks. Is there any reason why the delivery has been pushed back to 8 weeks?

麥可：你知道我們去年有買過同樣的產品，可是那時候交期只有四個星期，為什麼現在變成八星期呢？

Zoe: Right, the thing is, there is a bit of delay on the raw material. We are also waiting for it to arrive before we can start to manufacture.

柔伊：嗯，事情是因為目前原材料的交期有點延誤，我們也還在等東西來才可以開始加工。

影子跟讀「短對話」

影子跟讀「短段落」

影子跟讀「長段落」

# 交期太長向廠商詢問原因－報價單＋星期＋客戶溝通

▶▶ 「短對話」填空練習 🎧 MP3 007

　　除了前面的**「影子跟讀短對話練習」**，現在試著在聽完對話後，完成下列對話中填空部分，從中強化生活場景中常見的字彙以及拼字能力，答案的話請參照前面的對話喔！

| | |
|---|---|
| Michael: Hi Zoe, thanks for your _____. I did _____ something _____, and I thought I'd better check with you again. | 麥可：柔伊你好，謝謝你的報價，報價單有點不尋常，我想我最好再跟你確認一次。 |
| Zoe: Of course. You are referring to the _____ I sent _____ if I am not wrong? | 柔伊：當然，如果我沒想錯的話，你是指我昨天傳的那張嗎？ |
| Michael: Yeah, that's it. | 麥可：是的，沒錯。 |

Zoe: Oh... what is wrong with it?

柔伊：噢…是哪裡有問題呢？

Michael: You know we ordered the same thing ____ _____, but the _____ was only _____. Is there any _____ why the _____ has been pushed back to _____?

麥可：你知道我們去年有買過同樣的產品，可是那時候交期只有四個星期，為什麼現在變成八星期呢？

Zoe: Right, the thing is, there is a bit of _____ on the _____. We are also waiting for it to arrive before we can start to ____ _____.

柔伊：嗯，事情是因為目前原材料的交期有點延誤，我們也還在等東西來才可以開始加工。

影子跟讀「短對話」

影子跟讀「短段落」

影子跟讀「長段落」

45

# 替代品再次確認－
# 報價單＋型號＋產品

▶▶ 影子跟讀「短對話」練習　🎧 MP3 008

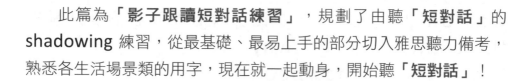

　　此篇為**「影子跟讀短對話練習」**，規劃了由聽**「短對話」**的 shadowing 練習，從最基礎、最易上手的部分切入雅思聽力備考，熟悉各生活場景類的用字，現在就一起動身，開始聽**「短對話」**！

Sandra: Hello Thomas. Thank you for your quotation. I noticed the part number is not what we enquired for, and it was not specified on the quotation. Is this a replacement?

珊卓：湯瑪士您好，謝謝你的報價單，可是我發現你報的型號跟我們詢價的不一樣，而且報價單上沒有特別註明，這是替代品嗎？

Thomas: It is actually an equivalent from a different maker, but the specification is the same as the part that you enquired for. It is

湯瑪士：那其實是不同製造商生產的同等品，規格跟你詢價的商品是一樣的，可是價格比原廠漢威公司的便宜了三成。

30% cheaper than the original Honeywell one.

Sandra: Well, luckily double checked with you before I send the quotation to the client. Can you send me another quotation for the original part, please? I will mention to the end user about the price difference to see if they are willing to switch to the equivalent.

珊卓：嗯，還好我在報價給客戶之前有跟你再次查證，你可以報價一個原廠的產品給我嗎？我會跟使用客戶提一下價格的區別，看看他們是不是願意用同等品。

影子跟讀「短對話」

影子跟讀「短段落」

影子跟讀「長段落」

# 替代品再次確認－報價單＋型號＋產品

▶▶「短對話」填空練習　 MP3 008

除了前面的「**影子跟讀短對話練習**」，現在試著在聽完對話後，完成下列對話中填空部分，從中強化生活場景中常見的字彙以及拼字能力，答案的話請參照前面的對話喔！

---

Sandra: Hello Thomas. Thank you for your quotation. I noticed the _____ is not what we enquired for, and it was not _____ on the quotation. Is this a _____?

珊卓：湯瑪士您好，謝謝你的報價單，可是我發現你報的型號跟我們詢價的不一樣，而且報價單上沒有特別註明，這是替代品嗎？

Thomas: It is actually an _____ from a _____ maker, but the _____ is the same as the part that you enquired for. It is _____ than the _____

湯瑪士：那其實是不同製造商生產的同等品，規格跟你詢價的商品是一樣的，可是價格比原廠漢威公司的便宜了三成。

Honeywell one.

Sandra: Well, luckily double checked with you before I send the quotation to the _____. Can you send me another quotation for the original part, please? I will _____ to the _____ ____ about the _____ to see if they are willing to _____ to the _____ __.

珊卓：嗯，還好我在報價給客戶之前有跟你再次查證，你可以報價一個原廠的產品給我嗎？我會跟使用客戶提一下價格的區別，看看他們是不是願意用同等品。

# 下單後要追加數量－數字＋運費＋折扣

▶▶ 影子跟讀「短對話」練習　🎧 MP3 009

此篇為「影子跟讀短對話練習」，規劃了由聽「短對話」的 shadowing 練習，從最基礎、最易上手的部分切入雅思聽力備考，熟悉各生活場景類的用字，現在就一起動身，開始聽「短對話」！

Claire: Hey John, you know that purchase order I sent two days ago for 500 packets of glue. Is it too late to change it to 1000 packets?

克萊兒：你好約翰，你知道我兩天前傳過去的那張 500 包黏著劑的那張訂單，我可以改成訂 1000 包嗎？

John: Right, I was just working on the order confirmation for you. You can change it to 1000 packets if you want.

約翰：喔！這樣啊！我剛剛才在處理你的訂單確認書，要改成 1000 包的話，沒有問題啊。

Claire: Thanks, but I just want to double check whether the delivery remains the same as 2 weeks. We would like to consolidate into one shipment to save the shipping cost.

克萊兒：好的，謝謝，可是我想再跟你確認一次這樣的話交期還是維持兩個星期嗎？我們想要跟之前的 500 包併貨一起出，這樣可以省一筆運費。

John: Let me check our inventory list. Well, I can ship all 1000 packets for you in 3 weeks, would it be ok?

約翰：讓我看一下我們的庫存表，這樣的話我們最快要三個星期的時間才能幫你出貨總計 1000 包的量，這樣可以接受嗎？

Claire: That would be great. In that case are we entitled to the quantity discount?

克萊兒：這樣沒問題，如果是這樣的話，那你們是不是會給我數量折扣？

John: Of course you are.

約翰：當然可以。

影子跟讀「短對話」

影子跟讀「短段落」

影子跟讀「長段落」

# 下單後要追加數量－數字＋運費＋折扣

▶▶ 「短對話」填空練習　🎧 MP3 009

除了前面的**「影子跟讀短對話練習」**，現在試著在聽完對話後，完成下列對話中填空部分，從中強化生活場景中常見的字彙以及拼字能力，答案的話請參照前面的對話喔！

Claire: Hey John, you know that _____ I sent __ _____ ago for _____ packets of _____. Is it too late to change it to ____ _____ packets?

克萊兒：你好約翰，你知道我兩天前傳過去的那張 500 包黏著劑的那張訂單，我可以改成訂 1000 包嗎？

John: Right, I was just working on the _____ for you. You can change it to 1000 packets if you want.

約翰：喔！這樣啊！我剛剛才在處理你的訂單確認書，要改成 1000 包的話，沒有問題啊。

Claire: Thanks, but I just want to _____ whether the _____ remains the same as _____. We would like to _____ into one _____ to save the _____.

克萊兒：好的，謝謝，可是我想再跟你確認一次這樣的話交期還是維持兩個星期嗎？我們想要跟之前的 500 包併貨一起出，這樣可以省一筆運費。

John: Let me check our _____. Well, I can ship all 1000 packets for you in _____, would it be ok?

約翰：讓我看一下我們的庫存表，這樣的話我們最快要三個星期的時間才能幫你出貨總計 1000 包的量，這樣可以接受嗎？

Claire: That would be great. In that case are we _____ to the _____?

克萊兒：這樣沒問題，如果是這樣的話，那你們是不是會給我數量折扣？

John: Of course, you are.

約翰：當然可以。

影子跟讀「短對話」

影子跟讀「短段落」

影子跟讀「長段落」

# 下單後發現錯誤—訂單＋客戶溝通＋電壓規格

▶▶ 影子跟讀「短對話」練習　🎧 MP3 010

　　此篇為**「影子跟讀短對話練習」**，規劃了由聽**「短對話」**的 shadowing 練習，從最基礎、最易上手的部分切入雅思聽力備考，熟悉各生活場景類的用字，現在就一起動身，開始聽**「短對話」**！

Jenny: Hello Jimmy, I have an emergency I hope you can help me. Can you put the purchase order that I sent last week on hold for the time being? I just realized the voltage might not be correct, and I have to check with the end user again.

珍妮：阿蘭娜你好，我有件急事需要你的幫忙，你可不可以把我上星期傳過去的訂單先暫停處理？我剛剛發現電壓好像不對，可是我必須再跟客戶確認一次。

Jimmy: Right, I would have to contact the manufactur-

吉米：這樣啊，我可能要先問一下製造商看是不是

er and see whether that is possible. I can't guarantee anything at this stage, but I will try my best. When do you think you can get back to me about the correct voltage?

可以先暫停，可是我不能保證一定可以。你什麼時候可以跟我確定電壓的規格？

Jenny: I will do it first thing tomorrow for sure. Thanks for trying. I hope I am not in too much trouble.

珍妮：我明天早上會優先處理，謝謝你的好意，希望我沒有闖大禍。

影子跟讀「短對話」

影子跟讀「短段落」

影子跟讀「長段落」

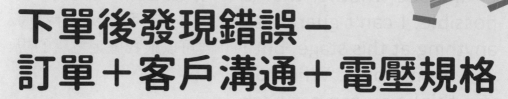

# 下單後發現錯誤－訂單＋客戶溝通＋電壓規格

▶▶ 「短對話」填空練習　🎧 MP3 010

　　除了前面的「**影子跟讀短對話練習**」，現在試著在聽完對話後，完成下列對話中填空部分，從中強化生活場景中常見的字彙以及拼字能力，答案的話請參照前面的對話喔！

Jenny: Hello Jimmy, I have an _____ I hope you can help me. Can you put the _____ that I sent __ _____ on hold for the time being? I just realized the _____ might not be correct, and I have to check with the _____ again.

珍妮：阿蘭娜你好，我有件急事需要你的幫忙，你可不可以把我上星期傳過去的訂單先暫停處理？我剛剛發現電壓好像不對，可是我必須再跟客戶確認一次。

Jimmy: Right, I would have to _____ the _____ and see whether that is possible. I can't _____

吉米：這樣啊，我可能要先問一下製造商看是不是可以先暫停，可是我不能保證一定可以。你什麼時

56

anything at this stage, but I will try my best. When do you think you can get back to me about the _____ voltage?

候可以跟我確定電壓的規格？

Jenny: I will do it first thing _____ for sure. Thanks for trying. I hope I am not in too _____.

珍妮：我明天早上會優先處理，謝謝你的好意，希望我沒有闖大禍。

# 提醒合約回傳－訂單編號＋日期＋月份

▶ 影子跟讀「短對話」練習　🎧 MP3 011

　　此篇為「影子跟讀短對話練習」，規劃了由聽「短對話」的 shadowing 練習，從最基礎、最易上手的部分切入雅思聽力備考，熟悉各生活場景類的用字，現在就一起動身，開始聽「短對話」！

Jeremy: Hello, this is Jeremy calling from Tai-Guang trading company in Taiwan. I was wondering whether you have received our purchase order number PO100165 dated 13th March 2017.

傑瑞米：您好，我是台灣台光貿易公司的崔西，我想請問一下您有沒有收到我們 2017 年 3 月 13 號傳的訂單呢？訂單號碼是 PO100165。

Belinda: Let me check my files. Was it on 13th March?

柏琳達：讓我看一下我的檔案，你是說 3 月 13 號傳的嗎？

Jeremy: Yes, it was, and we are still waiting for your order confirmation.

傑瑞米：是的，沒錯。我們一直還在等妳的訂單確認書。

Belinda: Right, is that what you are calling about? Sorry for the delay. I will be on to it, and you should have it by this afternoon.

柏琳達：好的，請問你特別打電話過來是這個原因嗎？很抱歉耽誤到你的時間，我會馬上處理，你應該今天下午就會收到。

Jeremy: Thanks for that. Can you also attach a copy of your bank detail please? We haven't had it on record.

傑瑞米：很謝謝你，可以麻煩你順便傳一份你的匯款帳號給我嗎？我們目前還沒有資料可以留底。

Belinda: Sure thing.

柏琳達：沒問題。

# 提醒合約回傳－ 訂單編號＋日期＋月份

▶▶ 「短對話」填空練習　🎧 MP3 011

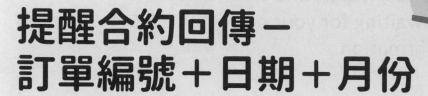

　　除了前面的**「影子跟讀短對話練習」**，現在試著在聽完對話後，完成下列對話中填空部分，從中強化生活場景中常見的字彙以及拼字能力，答案的話請參照前面的對話喔！

Jeremy: Hello, this is Jeremy calling from Tai-Guang trading ＿＿＿＿ in ＿＿＿ ＿＿. I was wondering whether you have received our purchase ＿＿＿＿ number ＿＿＿＿ dated ＿ ＿＿＿＿.

傑瑞米：您好，我是台灣台光貿易公司的崔西，我想請問一下您有沒有收到我們 2017 年 3 月 13 號傳的訂單呢？訂單號碼是 PO100165。

Belinda: Let me check my ＿＿＿＿. Was it on 13th ＿ ＿＿＿＿?

柏琳達：讓我看一下我的檔案，你是說 3 月 13 號傳的嗎？

Jeremy: Yes, it was, and we are still waiting for your order _____.

傑瑞米：是的，沒錯。我們一直還在等妳的訂單確認書。

Belinda: Right, is that what you are calling about? Sorry for the _____. I will be on to it, and you should have it by this _____.

柏琳達：好的，請問你特別打電話過來是這個原因嗎？很抱歉耽誤到你的時間，我會馬上處理，你應該今天下午就會收到。

Jeremy: Thanks for that. Can you also attach a _____ of your _____ _____ please? We haven't had it on _____.

傑瑞米：很謝謝你，可以麻煩你順便傳一份你的匯款帳號給我嗎？我們目前還沒有資料可以留底。

Belinda: Sure thing.

柏琳達：沒問題。

影子跟讀「短對話」

影子跟讀「短段落」

影子跟讀「長段落」

# 提醒付款條件－
# 訂單編號＋日期＋月份

▶▶ 影子跟讀「短對話」練習 🎧 MP3 012

　　此篇為**「影子跟讀短對話練習」**，規劃了由聽**「短對話」**的 shadowing 練習，從最基礎、最易上手的部分切入雅思聽力備考，熟悉各生活場景類的用字，現在就一起動身，開始聽**「短對話」**！

Jason: Hello, this is Jason calling from CK trading company in Taiwan. I am ringing regarding an order we received at the beginning of this month from Sue. I was wondering whether I can have a word with her, please?

傑森：您好，我是台灣 CK 貿易公司的傑森，我有些關於貴公司這個月初訂單的問題要找一下蘇。

Nina: Unfortunately, she is in a meeting at the moment. Can I take a mes-

妮娜：不好意思她目前正在開會，您要留話嗎？

sage?

Jason: Sure, I would like to check with her whether she put in a request for the down payment to be processed yet. Your order number is 0900234 dated 12th Jan 2017, and the down payment amount is USD 300. Please note the order will only be processed upon receipt of payment.

傑森：好的麻煩你，我想跟她確認一下她有沒有跟會計交代要匯錢的事。貴公司的訂單號碼是0900234，日期是 2017 年的 1 月 12 日。訂金的金額是美金三百塊。麻煩請提醒他訂單要收到訂金之後才會開始處理。

# 提醒付款條件－
# 訂單編號＋日期＋月份

▶▶ 「短對話」填空練習 🎧 MP3 012

除了前面的**「影子跟讀短對話練習」**，現在試著在聽完對話後，完成下列對話中填空部分，從中強化生活場景中常見的字彙以及拼字能力，答案的話請參照前面的對話喔！

Jason: Hello, this is Jason ___ _____ from CK trading __ _____ in _____. I am ringing regarding an order we _____ at the beginning of this _____ from Sue. I was wondering whether I can have _____ ___ with her, please?

傑森：您好，我是台灣 CK 貿易公司的傑森，我有些關於貴公司這個月初訂單的問題要找一下蘇。

Nina: Unfortunately, she is in a _____ at the moment. Can I take a _____ __?

妮娜：不好意思她目前正在開會，您要留話嗎？

Jason: Sure, I would like to check with her whether she put in a _____ for the _____ to be _____ yet. Your order number is _____ dated _____, and the _____ amount is USD _____. Please _____ the order will only be processed upon _____ of payment.

傑森：好的麻煩你，我想跟她確認一下她有沒有跟會計交代要匯錢的事。貴公司的訂單號碼是 0900234，日期是 2017 年的 1 月 12 日。訂金的金額是美金三百塊。麻煩請提醒他訂單要收到訂金之後才會開始處理。

影子跟讀「短對話」

影子跟讀「短段落」

影子跟讀「長段落」

# 提醒付款條件－
# 客戶溝通＋付款條件

▶▶ 影子跟讀「短對話」練習　🎧 MP3 013

　　此篇為**「影子跟讀短對話練習」**，規劃了由聽**「短對話」**的 shadowing 練習，從最基礎、最易上手的部分切入雅思聽力備考，熟悉各生活場景類的用字，現在就一起動身，開始聽**「短對話」**！

| | |
|---|---|
| Chris: Hello Miranda, if it's not too much to ask, I am hoping that you can do us a favor. | 克里斯：你好，瑪琳達，我希望這不會太麻煩你，我有事要拜託你。 |
| Miranda: Okay. What is it? | 瑪琳達：好，你說說看。 |
| Chris: Well, the business is a bit slow in the past few months. We are having a bit of cash flow issues. I | 克里斯：是因為這幾個月生意比較不好，我們的現金有點周轉不靈，我是想問妳我們可不可以研商一 |

was just wondering wheth-er we could come out with new payment terms.

下是不是可以改一下付款條件。

Miranda: Hmmm, I would have to ask my boss. You know it is purely his call. Just curious, what kind of payment terms are you proposing?

瑪琳達：這個嘛，我要跟我老闆商量一下，你知道這種事都是他決定。只是問一下，你是想要怎麼改？

Chris: If you can put in a good word for us and ex-tend the payment cycle from 60 days to 90 days, then it would be really helpful.

克里斯：如果你可以幫我們跟老闆求個情，讓他同意把 60 天延長為 90 天那就太好了。

影子跟讀「短對話」

影子跟讀「短段落」

影子跟讀「長段落」

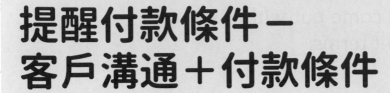

# 提醒付款條件－
# 客戶溝通＋付款條件

▶▶「短對話」填空練習　🎧 MP3 013

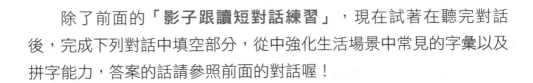

除了前面的「**影子跟讀短對話練習**」，現在試著在聽完對話後，完成下列對話中填空部分，從中強化生活場景中常見的字彙以及拼字能力，答案的話請參照前面的對話喔！

| | |
|---|---|
| Chris: Hello Miranda, if it's not too much to ask, I am hoping that you can do us a _____. | 克里斯：你好，瑪琳達，我希望這不會太麻煩你，我有事要拜託你。 |
| Miranda: Okay. What is it? | 瑪琳達：好，你說說看。 |
| Chris: Well, the _____ is a bit _____ in the past few months. We are having a bit of _____ issues. I was just wondering whether we could come | 克里斯：是因為這幾個月生意比較不好，我們的現金有點周轉不靈，我是想問妳我們可不可以研商一下是不是可以改一下付款條件。 |

out with _____ terms.

Miranda: Hmmm, I would have to ask _____. You know it is purely his call. Just _____, what kind of _____ are you proposing?

瑪琳達：這個嘛，我要跟我老闆商量一下，你知道這種事都是他決定。只是問一下，你是想要怎麼改？

Chris: If you can put in a good word for us and _____ the _____ from _____ days to _____ days, then it would be really helpful.

克里斯：如果你可以幫我們跟老闆求個情，讓他同意把 60 天延長為 90 天那就太好了。

影子跟讀「短對話」

影子跟讀「短段落」

影子跟讀「長段落」

# 即將出貨，請客戶付清尾款－訂單編號＋訂金和尾款＋月份

▶▶ 影子跟讀「短對話」練習 🎧 MP3 014

此篇為**「影子跟讀短對話練習」**，規劃了由聽**「短對話」**的 shadowing 練習，從最基礎、最易上手的部分切入雅思聽力備考，熟悉各生活場景類的用字，現在就一起動身，開始聽**「短對話」**！

| | |
|---|---|
| Sarah: How are you, Justin? | 莎拉：你好嗎？賈斯汀？ |
| Justin: I am good, thanks! What can I do for you? | 賈斯汀：我很好，謝謝你，可以幫你什麼忙嗎？ |
| Sarah: Just a courtesy call to let you know the shipment is ready for your order number PP88938. The initial payment of USD 500 was received December | 莎拉：我打來是好意提醒你，你訂單 PP88938 的貨已經好了，我們去年十二月已經收了 500 美金的訂金，尾款還剩 1500 美金，可以麻煩你這幾天內 |

last year and the remaining balance is USD 1500. Would you be able to arrange the payment for us in the next few days if possible?

幫我們安排付款嗎？

Justin: Sure, not a problem, just do me a favor, can you send us a shipping notice for record keeping purposes, and I will forward it to the accounts for you.

賈斯丁：當然，沒有問題。可以請你幫我個忙嗎，麻煩你傳一張簡短的出貨通知給我做紀錄嗎？我會交代給會計部門。

影子跟讀「短對話」

影子跟讀「短段落」

影子跟讀「長段落」

# 即將出貨，請客戶付清尾款－訂單編號＋訂金和尾款＋月份

▶▶ 「短對話」填空練習 🎧 MP3 014

　　除了前面的「**影子跟讀短對話練習**」，現在試著在聽完對話後，完成下列對話中填空部分，從中強化生活場景中常見的字彙以及拼字能力，答案的話請參照前面的對話喔！

| | |
|---|---|
| Sarah: How are you, Justin? | 莎拉：你好嗎？賈斯汀？ |
| Justin: I am good, thanks! What can I do for you? | 賈斯汀：我很好，謝謝你，可以幫你什麼忙嗎？ |
| Sarah: Just a _____ call to let you know the _____ is ready for your order number _____. The initial _____ of USD _____ was received _____ last year and the _____ is USD _____. | 莎拉：我打來是好意提醒你，你訂單 PP88938 的貨已經好了，我們去年十二月已經收了 500 美金的訂金，尾款還剩 1500 美金，可以麻煩你這幾天內幫我們安排付款嗎？ |

Would you be able to ____ _____ the payment for us in the next _____ if possible?

Justin: Sure, not a problem, just do me a favor, can you send us a shipping _____ __ for _____ keeping purposes, and I will forward it to the _____ for you.

賈斯丁：當然，沒有問題。可以請你幫我個忙嗎，麻煩你傳一張簡短的出貨通知給我做紀錄嗎？我會交代給會計部門。

影子跟讀「短對話」

影子跟讀「短段落」

影子跟讀「長段落」

# 匯款單／會計部門－尾款＋星期＋匯款水單

▶▶ 影子跟讀「短對話」練習 🎧 MP3 015

　　此篇為「影子跟讀短對話練習」，規劃了由聽「短對話」的 shadowing 練習，從最基礎、最易上手的部分切入雅思聽力備考，熟悉各生活場景類的用字，現在就一起動身，開始聽「短對話」！

Justin: Hello Sarah, I am calling to let you know the payment has been made on Monday, and you should have it by now.

賈斯丁：你好莎拉，我是打來通知你，尾款已經在星期一匯過去了，你應該已經收到了吧？

Sarah: Oh, thanks for that. would you be able to send me the remittance advice, so we can track the payment with our bank, please?

莎拉：喔！謝謝你幫我處理，你可以把匯款水單傳給我嗎？這樣我可以跟銀行追蹤款項。

Justin: Not a problem. Just to let you know we did instruct the bank to cover the bank charge as well. You should receive the exact amount of USD1500.

賈斯丁：沒問題，順便跟你說我有交代銀行手續費的部份我們會負責，你會收到整數 1500 美金。

Sarah: That's great！The Accounting Department will be impressed. The shipment is ready to go. I will contact the courier, and the shipment will be on its way to you this afternoon.

莎拉：太好了，我們會計會很高興。貨已經好了，我會叫快遞來收貨，下午就會出貨給你。

# 匯款單／會計部門－尾款＋星期＋匯款水單

▶▶ 「短對話」填空練習 🎧 MP3 015

除了前面的**「影子跟讀短對話練習」**，現在試著在聽完對話後，完成下列對話中填空部分，從中強化生活場景中常見的字彙以及拼字能力，答案的話請參照前面的對話喔！

Justin: Hello Sarah, I am calling to let you know the _____ has been made on _____, and you should have it _____.

賈斯丁：你好莎拉，我是打來通知你，尾款已經在星期一匯過去了，你應該已經收到了吧？

Sarah: Oh, thanks for that. would you be able to send me the _____ advice, so we can track the payment with our bank, please?

莎拉：喔！謝謝你幫我處理，你可以把匯款水單傳給我嗎？這樣我可以跟銀行追蹤款項。

Justin: Not a problem. Just to let you know we did ____ _____ the _____ to cover the _____ as well. You should receive the ____ _____ of USD_____.

賈斯丁：沒問題，順便跟你説我有交代銀行手續費的部份我們會負責，你會收到整數 1500 美金。

Sarah: That's great！The __ _____ will be _____. The _____ is ready to go. I will contact the _____ ____, and the _____ will be on its way to you this __ _____.

莎拉：太好了，我們會計會很高興。貨已經好了，我會叫快遞來收貨，下午就會出貨給你。

影子跟讀「短對話」

影子跟讀「短段落」

影子跟讀「長段落」

77

# 更改運送方式－
# 訂單編號＋資料＋費用

▶▶ 影子跟讀「短對話」練習 🎧 MP3 016

此篇為**「影子跟讀短對話練習」**，規劃了由聽**「短對話」**的 shadowing 練習，從最基礎、最易上手的部分切入雅思聽力備考，熟悉各生活場景類的用字，現在就一起動身，開始聽**「短對話」**！

Pheony: Hi Johnny, I need to make an amendment regarding the shipping method for our PO number 9900384. I'll just quickly run through it with you before I send the new shipping details to you.

費昂妮：強尼您好，我需要更改訂單號碼 9900384 的運送方式，我先口頭跟你解釋一下再把新運送方式的資料傳給你。

Johnny: Sure, go ahead.

強尼：好的，請說。

Pheony: We were going to use your contracted forwarder, but we decided to go with our courier instead since it works out about the same but much faster.

費昂妮：我們本來是要用你們簽約的運送公司，可是我們現在決定要用我們自己的快遞公司去收貨，算起來費用差不多但是比較快。

Johnny: Sure, we can do that, but you know you are still liable for the handling charge.

強尼：當然，我們可以處理，可是要提醒你，這樣的話你還是要付訂單處理費。

Pheony: Yes, I do.

費昂妮：嗯，我知道。

Johnny: Ok then, I will revise the order confirmation once I got the courier details from you.

強尼：好，那等你傳資料過來之後，我在幫你改訂單確認書。

影子跟讀「短對話」

影子跟讀「短段落」

影子跟讀「長段落」

# 更改運送方式－ 訂單編號＋資料＋費用

▶▶ 「短對話」填空練習 🎧 MP3 016

除了前面的**「影子跟讀短對話練習」**，現在試著在聽完對話後，完成下列對話中填空部分，從中強化生活場景中常見的字彙以及拼字能力，答案的話請參照前面的對話喔！

Pheony: Hi Johnny, I need to make an _____ regarding the shipping _____ for our PO number _____. I'll just quickly run through it with you before I send the new _____ to you.

費昂妮：強尼您好，我需要更改訂單號碼 9900384 的運送方式，我先口頭跟你解釋一下再把新運送方式的資料傳給你。

Johnny: Sure, go ahead.

強尼：好的，請説。

Pheony: We were going to use your _____, but we

費昂妮：我們本來是要用你們簽約的運送公司，可

decided to go with our _____ _____ instead since it works out about the same but much faster.

是我們現在決定要用我們自己的快遞公司去收貨，算起來費用差不多但是比較快。

Johnny: Sure, we can do that, but you know you are still liable for the _____ __.

強尼：當然，我們可以處理，可是要提醒你，這樣的話你還是要付訂單處理費。

Pheony: Yes, I do.

費昂妮：嗯，我知道。

Johnny: Ok then, I will revise the _____ once I got the _____ details from you.

強尼：好，那等你傳資料過來之後，我在幫你改訂單確認書。

影子跟讀「短對話」

影子跟讀「短段落」

影子跟讀「長段落」

# 有急用請廠商分批出貨－訂單編號＋數字＋星期

▶▶ 影子跟讀「短對話」練習 🎧 MP3 017

　　此篇為「**影子跟讀短對話練習**」，規劃了由聽「**短對話**」的 shadowing 練習，從最基礎、最易上手的部分切入雅思聽力備考，熟悉各生活場景類的用字，現在就一起動身，開始聽「**短對話**」！

| | |
|---|---|
| Mei -Ling: Hello Harrison. I was wondering whether you could help me out. I need to check the progress of one of our orders. | 美玲：哈里森您好，你能不能夠幫我一個忙，我想詢問一下我們其中一個訂單的進度。 |
| Harrison: Of course, which order are you referring to? | 哈里森：沒問題，你說的是哪一個訂單？ |
| Mei -Ling: The PO number is KK12330. It was for 10 | 美玲：我們的訂單號碼是 KK12330，是十個汽缸。 |

cylinders.

Harrison: Let me see... Well the order won't be ready for another 3 weeks.

哈里森：我看一下，嗯，這個訂單還有三個星期才能供貨。

Mei-Ling: I know, but we have a situation here. One o f the production lines is down, and the end user desperately needs one to get their machine up and running. Would you be able to check whether you can have any in stock and available for shipping immediately? The rest can wait until then.

美玲：我知道，可是我們現在有問題，客戶其中一台的機台壞了，現在使用者急需一個汽缸來替換，你能不能蓋查一下你們有沒有一個現貨可以馬上出貨給我們？其他九個可以等到三個禮拜後再出。

影子跟讀「短對話」

影子跟讀「短段落」

影子跟讀「長段落」

*83*

# 有急用請廠商分批出貨－訂單編號＋數字＋星期

▶▶ 「短對話」填空練習　🎧 MP3 017

　　除了前面的**「影子跟讀短對話練習」**，現在試著在聽完對話後，完成下列對話中填空部分，從中強化生活場景中常見的字彙以及拼字能力，答案的話請參照前面的對話喔！

Mei -Ling: Hello Harrison. I was wondering whether you could help me out. I need to _____ the _____ of one of our orders.

美玲：哈里森您好，你能不能夠幫我一個忙，我想詢問一下我們其中一個訂單的進度。

Harrison: Of course, which order are you referring to?

哈里森：沒問題，你説的是哪一個訂單？

Mei -Ling: The PO number is _____. It was for _____.

美玲：我們的訂單號碼是KK12330，是十個汽缸。

Harrison: Let me see... Well the _____ won't be ready for another _____.

哈里森：我看一下，嗯，這個訂單還有三個星期才能供貨。

Mei-Ling: I know, but we have a _____ here. One o f the _____ lines is down, and the end user __ _____ needs one to get their _____ up and running. Would you be able to check whether you can have any _____ and available for _____ immediately? _____ can wait until then.

美玲：我知道，可是我們現在有問題，客戶其中一台的機台壞了，現在使用者急需一個汽缸來替換，你能不能蓋查一下你們有沒有一個現貨可以馬上出貨給我們？其他九個可以等到三個禮拜後再出。

# 確認運送方式－訂單編號＋規格＋重量

▶ 影子跟讀「短對話」練習 🎧 MP3 018

　　此篇為「影子跟讀短對話練習」，規劃了由聽「短對話」的 shadowing 練習，從最基礎、最易上手的部分切入雅思聽力備考，熟悉各生活場景類的用字，現在就一起動身，開始聽「短對話」！

Fred: Hi Emma, just to let you know your order number 835001 is ready to be picked up. I just noticed that you haven't specified the shipping method on your PO, do you want us to courier it or send it via a forwarder.

佛萊德：艾瑪您好，我是想通知您貴公司的 835001 號訂單已經可以出貨了，可是我發現你們訂單上並沒有註明要用何種運送方式，您想要用快遞出貨還是要用海運出貨呢？

Emma: Right, my apology. Please hold on a second, let me check. Do you hap-

艾瑪：喔，這樣啊，很抱歉我疏忽了。請您稍等一下，我來看看。請問貨品

影子跟讀「短對話」

影子跟讀「短段落」

影子跟讀「長段落」

pen to know the dimensions of the package?

的外包裝的尺寸是多少？

Fred: Yes, it is 120×90×50 cm, and the weight is approximately 25 kilos.

佛萊德：嗯，是 120×90×50 公分，總重大概是 25 公斤。

Emma: In that case, please use our CPS to collect account. Our account number is: XX659922.

艾瑪：這樣的話，麻煩您用我們 CPS 快遞的對方付款帳號來出貨，帳號是：XX659922。

# 確認運送方式－訂單編號＋規格＋重量

▶▶「短對話」填空練習　🎧 MP3 018

除了前面的**「影子跟讀短對話練習」**，現在試著在聽完對話後，完成下列對話中填空部分，從中強化生活場景中常見的字彙以及拼字能力，答案的話請參照前面的對話喔！

Fred: Hi Emma, just to let you know your order number _____ is ready to be picked up. I just noticed that you haven't _____ the _____ method on your PO, do you want us to _____ it or send it via a _____.

佛萊德：艾瑪您好，我是想通知您貴公司的 835001 號訂單已經可以出貨了，可是我發現你們訂單上並沒有註明要用何種運送方式，您想要用快遞出貨還是要用海運出貨呢？

Emma: Right, my apology. Please hold on a second, let me check. Do you happen to know the _____

艾瑪：喔，這樣啊，很抱歉我疏忽了。請您稍等一下，我來看看。請問貨品的外包裝的尺寸是多少？

of the _____ ?

Fred: Yes, it is _____ cm, and the _____ is approximately _____ .

佛萊德：嗯，是 120×90×50 公分，總重大概是 25 公斤。

Emma: In that case, please use our CPS to _____ account. Our _____ number is: _____ .

艾瑪：這樣的話，麻煩您用我們 CPS 快遞的對方付款帳號來出貨，帳號是：XX659922。

影子跟讀「短對話」

影子跟讀「短段落」

影子跟讀「長段落」

# 收到錯誤的商品，要求更換－訂單＋方向＋年份

▶ 影子跟讀「短對話」練習　🎧 MP3 019

此篇為「影子跟讀短對話練習」，規劃了由聽「短對話」的 shadowing 練習，從最基礎、最易上手的部分切入雅思聽力備考，熟悉各生活場景類的用字，現在就一起動身，開始聽「短對話」！

Terry: Hello Lucy, there is a problem here. We received the conveyor belt yesterday, but the design is wrong. The build-in magnet was supposed to be on the right side, but it was on the left.

泰瑞：露西您好，我們現在有個問題，輸送帶昨天收到了，可是設計上有錯。裡面內建的磁鐵應該是要在右邊，不是左邊。

Lucy: Right, let me check the order. Did you point out which side the magnet is meant to be on?

露西：這樣啊，讓我檢查一下你們的訂單，你有在訂單上有特別註明嗎？

Terry: Yes, we did. This conveyor belt is meant to be the replacement for the one we ordered 3 years ago. With the magnet on the wrong side, there is no way we can use this.

泰瑞：當然有，我們三年前訂過一樣的輸送帶，而這個新的輸送帶是要來更換舊的這個。所以如果磁鐵方向做錯，我們就沒辦法用這個東西了。

Lucy: Well, I would have to check with the engineering department and see what we can do. Do you mind shipping the conveyor back?

露西：我知道了，我會跟工程部門討論，看能怎麼處理。你介意把東西退回來嗎？

影子跟讀「短對話」

影子跟讀「短段落」

影子跟讀「長段落」

# 收到錯誤的商品，要求更換－訂單＋方向＋年份

▶▶ 「短對話」填空練習　🎧 MP3 019

除了前面的**「影子跟讀短對話練習」**，現在試著在聽完對話後，完成下列對話中填空部分，從中強化生活場景中常見的字彙以及拼字能力，答案的話請參照前面的對話喔！

Terry: Hello Lucy, there is a _____ here. We received the _____ yesterday, but the _____ is wrong. The build-in _____ was supposed to be on the _____ side, but it was on the _____.

泰瑞：露西您好，我們現在有個問題，輸送帶昨天收到了，可是設計上有錯。裡面內建的磁鐵應該是要在右邊，不是左邊。

Lucy: Right, let me check the _____. Did you point out which _____ the magnet is meant to be on?

露西：這樣啊，讓我檢查一下你們的訂單，你有在訂單上有特別註明嗎？

Terry: Yes, we did. This _____ _____ is meant to be the __ _____ for the one we ordered _____. With the _____ on the wrong side, there is no way we can use this.

泰瑞：當然有，我們三年前訂過一樣的輸送帶，而這個新的輸送帶是要來更換舊的這個。所以如果磁鐵方向做錯，我們就沒辦法用這個東西了。

Lucy: Well, I would have to check with the _____ department and see what we can do. Do you mind __ _____ the _____ back?

露西：我知道了，我會跟工程部門討論，看能怎麼處理。你介意把東西退回來嗎？

影子跟讀「短對話」

影子跟讀「短段落」

影子跟讀「長段落」

# 運送過程損壞，向國外反應－數量＋產品更換＋運費

▶▶ 影子跟讀「短對話」練習　🎧 MP3 020

此篇為**「影子跟讀短對話練習」**，規劃了由聽**「短對話」**的 shadowing 練習，從最基礎、最易上手的部分切入雅思聽力備考，熟悉各生活場景類的用字，現在就一起動身，開始聽**「短對話」**！

Sam: Hello, Lyndsay, thanks for the shipment, we received it yesterday. But 1 of the temperature gauges is damaged. The protecting glass is broken, can you replace them?

山姆：琳希您好，謝謝你幫我們出貨，我們昨天收到了，可是其中的一個溫度計有破損，上面的保護鏡破掉了，你可以幫我們更換嗎？

Lyndsay: Just one out of ten? Yes, we can replace them, but we are not responsible for the additional shipping cost.

琳希：十個裡面破了一個嗎？沒問題，我們可以更換，可是額外的運費要你們自付。

Sam: Yes, I can understand that.

山姆：好，這個我了解。

Lyndsay: Can you arrange for the broken one to be returned, please?

琳希：可以麻煩你把破的那個寄回來嗎？

Sam: Definitely. Since I've got you one the phone, can you check whether you have 1 available for shipping immediately?

山姆：那當然，既然你在線上，我可以順便詢問一下你們是否有一個現貨可以馬上出？

Lyndsay: Unfortunately, we don't have any at the moment, but the next batch will be ready in two days. I can organize 1 to go out to you straight away if that helps.

琳希：不好意思沒有，可是下一批貨兩天後就會好，我可以馬上幫你寄個去如果你要的話。

Sam: That would be great.

山姆：好的，那麻煩你。

影子跟讀「短對話」

影子跟讀「短段落」

影子跟讀「長段落」

# 運送過程損壞，向國外反應－數量＋產品更換＋運費

▶▶ 「短對話」填空練習　🎧 MP3 020

除了前面的**「影子跟讀短對話練習」**，現在試著在聽完對話後，完成下列對話中填空部分，從中強化生活場景中常見的字彙以及拼字能力，答案的話請參照前面的對話喔！

Sam: Hello, Lyndsay, thanks for the _____, we received it _____. But 1 of the _____ gauges is _____. The _____ is broken, can you _____ them?

山姆：琳希您好，謝謝你幫我們出貨，我們昨天收到了，可是其中的一個溫度計有破損，上面的保護鏡破掉了，你可以幫我們更換嗎？

Lyndsay: Just one out of _____? Yes, we can replace them, but we are not responsible for the _____.

琳希：十個裡面破了一個嗎？沒問題，我們可以更換，可是額外的運費要你們自付。

Sam: Yes, I can understand

山姆：好，這個我了解。

that.

Lyndsay: Can you _____ _ for the _____ one to be returned, please?

琳希：可以麻煩你把破的那個寄回來嗎？

Sam: Definitely. Since I've got you one the _____, can you check whether you have _____ available for _____ immediate-ly?

山姆：那當然，既然你在線上，我可以順便詢問一下你們是否有一個現貨可以馬上出？

Lyndsay: Unfortunately, we don't have any at the mo-ment, but the next _____ _ will be ready in _____ __. I can organize 1 to go out to you _____ if that helps.

琳希：不好意思沒有，可是下一批貨兩天後就會好，我可以馬上幫你寄個去如果你要的話。

Sam: That would be great.

山姆：好的，那麻煩你。

# 海運航班接不上，無法準時交貨－地名＋日期＋月份

▶▶ 影子跟讀「短對話」練習　🎧 MP3 021

　　此篇為「影子跟讀短對話練習」，規劃了由聽「短對話」的 shadowing 練習，從最基礎、最易上手的部分切入雅思聽力備考，熟悉各生活場景類的用字，現在就一起動身，開始聽「短對話」！

Linda: Hi Jimmy, I just heard from the forwarder, the shipment was scheduled to arrive in Kaohsiung port on 25th Mar, but there is a delay in Singapore. Looks like the shipping vessel would hang around Singapore for extra 3-4 days.

琳達：吉米你好，我聽我們船運公司說貨輪本來是預計 3 月 25 日抵達高雄港，可是在新加坡有些問題耽誤了，看來可能在新加坡會多耽誤 3 到 4 天。

Jimmy: Right! Thanks for letting me know. I think extra 3 or 4 days would not

吉米：這樣啊！謝謝你通知我，如果只是三、四天那倒是還好，只要不要超

cause any problem, but if it is longer than a week, then we might be in trouble for missing the deadline.

過一個星期，因為我們可能會因延誤交期而有麻煩。

Linda: There is nothing we can do other than wait. I will keep an eye on this case, but I will keep you posted when I know more.

琳達：目前我們只能等，我會特別注意這個案子，但是有消息我會隨時跟你聯絡。

影子跟讀「短對話」

影子跟讀「短段落」

影子跟讀「長段落」

# 海運航班接不上，無法準時交貨－地名＋日期＋月份

▶▶ 「短對話」填空練習 🎧 MP3 021

除了前面的**「影子跟讀短對話練習」**，現在試著在聽完對話後，完成下列對話中填空部分，從中強化生活場景中常見的字彙以及拼字能力，答案的話請參照前面的對話喔！

Linda: Hi Jimmy, I just heard from the _____, the _____ was scheduled to arrive in _____ port on _____, but there is a _____ in _____. Looks like the _____ would hang around _____ for extra 3-4 days.

琳達：吉米你好，我聽我們船運公司説貨輪本來是預計 3 月 25 日抵達高雄港，可是在新加坡有些問題耽誤了，看來可能在新加坡會多耽誤 3 到 4 天。

Jimmy: Right! Thanks for letting me know. I think extra _____ days would not cause any problem, but

吉米：這樣啊！謝謝你通知我，如果只是三、四天那倒是還好，只要不要超過一個星期，因為我們可

if it is longer than _____
__, then we might be in trouble for missing the ____
_____.

能會因延誤交期而有麻煩。

Linda: There is nothing we can do other than wait. I will _____ on this case, but I will keep you posted when I know more.

**琳達：**目前我們只能等，我會特別注意這個案子，但是有消息我會隨時跟你聯絡。

影子跟讀「短對話」

影子跟讀「短段落」

影子跟讀「長段落」

# 收到的貨物與出貨單內容不符－訂單編號＋日期＋月份

▶▶ 影子跟讀「短對話」練習 🎧 MP3 022

此篇為**「影子跟讀短對話練習」**，規劃了由聽**「短對話」**的 shadowing 練習，從最基礎、最易上手的部分切入雅思聽力備考，熟悉各生活場景類的用字，現在就一起動身，開始聽**「短對話」**！

---

Michelle: Thanks for the shipment, but I think there is a problem. This is not the right order for us.

蜜雪兒：謝謝你的出貨，可是這批貨有點問題，這跟我們訂的貨不一樣。

Justin: Right, can you explain further, please?

賈斯丁：是嗎？可以說清楚一點嗎？

Michelle: Sure, do you have a copy of the packing list handy?

蜜雪兒：當然，你手邊有我們的出貨單嗎？

Justin: Just a minute, I will look it up. Here it is.

賈斯丁：稍等，我找一下，找到了。

Michelle: On the packing list it shows that we ordered a complete filter system which is housing plus a filter pad, but what we received is only a filter pad replacement. Can you please check your record and send us the filter housing ASAP please?

蜜雪兒：在出貨單上顯示我們訂的是整組的過濾器，就是過濾器再加上濾網，可是實際上貨物裡面只有濾網。你可以查一下你的出貨紀錄然後趕快補一個過濾器給我們嗎？

Justin: Ok, I will check with my coworker and let you know shortly.

賈斯丁：好的，我跟我的同事求證一下再跟你說。

影子跟讀「短對話」

影子跟讀「短段落」

影子跟讀「長段落」

# 收到的貨物與出貨單內容不符－訂單編號＋日期＋月份

▶▶ 「短對話」填空練習　🎧 MP3 022

除了前面的**「影子跟讀短對話練習」**，現在試著在聽完對話後，完成下列對話中填空部分，從中強化生活場景中常見的字彙以及拼字能力，答案的話請參照前面的對話喔！

| | |
|---|---|
| Michelle: Thanks for the shipment, but I think there is a _____. This is not the _____ for us. | 蜜雪兒：謝謝你的出貨，可是這批貨有點問題，這跟我們訂的貨不一樣。 |
| Justin: Right, can you explain further, please? | 賈斯丁：是嗎？可以說清楚一點嗎？ |
| Michelle: Sure, do you have a _____ of the packing list _____? | 蜜雪兒：當然，你手邊有我們的出貨單嗎？ |

Justin: Just a _____, I will look it up. Here it is.

賈斯丁：稍等，我找一下，找到了。

Michelle: On the _____ it shows that we ordered a _____ system which is housing plus a filter pad, but what we received is only a _____ pad replacement. Can you please check your _____ and send us the filter housing ASAP please?

蜜雪兒：在出貨單上顯示我們訂的是整組的過濾器，就是過濾器再加上濾網，可是實際上貨物裡面只有濾網。你可以查一下你的出貨紀錄然後趕快補一個過濾器給我們嗎？

Justin: Ok, I will check with my _____ and let you know _____.

賈斯丁：好的，我跟我的同事求證一下再跟你説。

# 供應商來訪－時間點＋日期＋月份

▶▶ 影子跟讀「短對話」練習　🎧 MP3 023

此篇為「影子跟讀短對話練習」，規劃了由聽「短對話」的 shadowing 練習，從最基礎、最易上手的部分切入雅思聽力備考，熟悉各生活場景類的用字，現在就一起動身，開始聽「短對話」！

Cherry: Hello Jason, I was wondering whether Mr. Tseng would be available at 10:00 on 5th of July. Mr. Robinson would like to have a meeting with him to discuss the Da-Ling project. I will send you the agenda shortly.

佳麗：你好，傑森，請問曾先生七月五日早上十點有空嗎？羅賓森先生想跟他討論一下大林專案，我晚一點把會議要討論的事項傳給你。

Jason: Let me check his schedule. He has a meeting booked with our sales man-

傑森：讓我看一下他的行程，嗯，他早上要跟我們的業務經理開會，羅賓森

ager that morning, is Mr. Robinson free that afternoon? Say 2 pm?

先生下午有空嗎？兩點好不好？

影子跟讀「短對話」

Cherry: He has a lunch meeting with someone else, and they should be done around 2 pm. Can you book him in for 3 pm then?

佳麗：他中午跟其他人有約，大概兩點會好，那約三點好嗎？

影子跟讀「短段落」

Jason: I sure can. Does he have a dinner plan? If not, I am sure Mr.Tseng would like to take him out for dinner.

傑森：當然可以，他晚餐有約人了嗎？不然曾先生想請他吃飯。

影子跟讀「長段落」

# 供應商來訪－時間點＋日期＋月份

▶▶ 「短對話」填空練習 🎧 MP3 023

除了前面的**「影子跟讀短對話練習」**，現在試著在聽完對話後，完成下列對話中填空部分，從中強化生活場景中常見的字彙以及拼字能力，答案的話請參照前面的對話喔！

---

Cherry: Hello Jason, I was wondering whether Mr. Tseng would be _____ at 10:00 on _____. Mr. Robinson would like to have a _____ with him to discuss the Da-Ling _____. I will send you the _____ shortly.

佳麗：你好，傑森，請問曾先生七月五日早上十點有空嗎？羅賓森先生想跟他討論一下大林專案，我晚一點把會議要討論的事項傳給你。

Jason: Let me check his _____. He has a meeting booked with our _____ that _____, is Mr. Rob-

傑森：讓我看一下他的行程，嗯，他早上要跟我們的業務經理開會，羅賓森先生下午有空嗎？兩點好

inson free that _____?
Say 2 pm?

不好？

Cherry: He has a _____
meeting with someone
else, and they should be
done around 2 pm. Can you
_____ him in for _____
____ then?

佳麗：他中午跟其他人有
約，大概兩點會好，那約
三點好嗎？

Jason: I sure can. Does he
have _____? If not, I
am sure Mr.Tseng would
like to take him out for ____
_____.

傑森：當然可以，他晚餐
有約人了嗎？不然曾先生
想請他吃飯。

# 飛機延誤需更改行程及接機－班機＋日期＋行程

▶ 影子跟讀「短對話」練習　🎧 MP3 024

　　此篇為「**影子跟讀短對話練習**」，規劃了由聽「**短對話**」的 shadowing 練習，從最基礎、最易上手的部分切入雅思聽力備考，熟悉各生活場景類的用字，現在就一起動身，開始聽「**短對話**」！

Tammy: Hi Frank, I am sorry for calling so late. I am calling to let you know that Mr. Rollings missed the connecting flight for tomorrow morning, and he won't get in until 11:00 am. Can you push the meeting back by a day and reschedule it to the day after?

潭美：你好法蘭克，很抱歉這麼晚打給你，我是想通知你羅倫斯先生在曼谷機場的班機沒接上，他們重新幫他訂了明天早上的飛機，可是他要早上 11 點才會到，可以麻煩你把原來的會議推遲一天改成後天嗎？

Frank: Thanks for letting me know. From what I can

法蘭克：謝謝你通知我，我記得吳先生後天有空，

recall, I think Mr. Wu would be free the day after. It should not be a problem. Can you let me know the flight number please? I will notify the driver, so he will be there to pick him up when he arrives.

應該沒有問題。可以告訴我他們班機號碼嗎？我會通知司機在他抵達機場時會去接他。

影子跟讀「短對話」

影子跟讀「短段落」

影子跟讀「長段落」

# 飛機延誤需更改行程及接機－班機＋日期＋行程

▶▶ 「短對話」填空練習 🎧 MP3 024

除了前面的**「影子跟讀短對話練習」**，現在試著在聽完對話後，完成下列對話中填空部分，從中強化生活場景中常見的字彙以及拼字能力，答案的話請參照前面的對話喔！

Tammy: Hi Frank, I am sorry for calling so late. I am calling to let you know that Mr. Rollings missed the __ _____ for _____ morning, and he won't get in until _____. Can you push the _____ back by a day and _____ it to the day after?

潭美：你好法蘭克，很抱歉這麼晚打給你，我是想通知你羅倫斯先生在曼谷機場的班機沒接上，他們重新幫他訂了明天早上的飛機，可是他要早上 11 點才會到，可以麻煩你把原來的會議推遲一天改成後天嗎？

Frank: Thanks for letting me know. From what I can _____, I think Mr. Wu

法蘭克：謝謝你通知我，我記得吳先生後天有空，應該沒有問題。可以告訴

would be _____ the day after. It should not be a _____. Can you let me know the _____ please? I will notify the _____, so he will be there to pick him up when he arrives.

我他們班機號碼嗎？我會通知司機在他抵達機場時會去接他。

# 討論會議中談論的事項執行進度－專案＋星期＋會議記錄

▶▶ 影子跟讀「短對話」練習　🎧 MP3 025

　　此篇為「影子跟讀短對話練習」，規劃了由聽「短對話」的 shadowing 練習，從最基礎、最易上手的部分切入雅思聽力備考，熟悉各生活場景類的用字，現在就一起動身，開始聽「短對話」！

Tammy: Hi Jimmy, has Mr. Wu spoken to you regarding the specifications of the Da-Ling project? Apparently, he told me Mr. Rollings will forward it to him.

潭美：蘇西您好，吳先生有沒有跟你說過關於大林專案的詳細計劃書？顯然，吳先生跟我提過，說羅斯先生會將專案轉交給他。

Jimmy: Yes, I am working on it at the moment. There are a few amendments that need to be done and Mr. Wu also wants to add a few things in it. I should have it

吉米：有的！我現在正在處理，不過還有點地方要修改，吳先生還有東西要新增，我應該下禮拜二就可以給你。

ready by next Tuesday.

Tammy: That would be great. Do you have a copy of the meeting minutes that I can have? Just in case I missed anything. | 潭美：那太好了，我可以順便跟你要一份會議紀錄嗎？我可以對照一下，怕我疏忽掉其他的東西。

Jimmy: Definitely, I will send it to you straight away. | 吉米：當然可以，這個我馬上就可以傳給你。

# 討論會議中談論的事項執行進度－專案＋星期＋會議記錄

▶▶ 「短對話」填空練習 🎧 MP3 025

除了前面的**「影子跟讀短對話練習」**，現在試著在聽完對話後，完成下列對話中填空部分，從中強化生活場景中常見的字彙以及拼字能力，答案的話請參照前面的對話喔！

Tammy: Hi Jimmy, has Mr. Wu spoken to you regarding the _____ of the Da-Ling _____? Apparently, he told me Mr. Rollings will _____ it to him.

潭美：蘇西您好，吳先生有沒有跟你說過關於大林專案的詳細計劃書？顯然，吳先生跟我提過，說羅斯先生會將專案轉交給他。

Jimmy: Yes, I am working on it at the _____. There are a few _____ that need to be done and Mr. Wu also wants to add a few things in it. I should

吉米：有的！我現在正在處理，不過還有點地方要修改，吳先生還有東西要新增，我應該下禮拜二就可以給你。

have it ready by _____ .

Tammy: That would be great. Do you have a _____ ____ of the _____ that I can have? Just in case I missed _____ .

潭美：那太好了，我可以順便跟你要一份會議紀錄嗎？我可以對照一下，怕我疏忽掉其他的東西。

Jimmy: Definitely, I will ____ _____ it to you straight away.

吉米：當然可以，這個我馬上就可以傳給你。

# 訪客的喜好／注意事項－餐廳＋餐點＋房間

▶▶ 影子跟讀「短對話」練習　🎧 MP3 026

此篇為「影子跟讀短對話練習」，規劃了由聽「短對話」的 shadowing 練習，從最基礎、最易上手的部分切入雅思聽力備考，熟悉各生活場景類的用字，現在就一起動身，開始聽「短對話」！

| | |
|---|---|
| Mark: Hey Belinda, I am making a reservation for lunch for Mr. Moss. Does he have any special dietary requirements? | 馬克：柏琳達您好，我現在要幫摩斯先生安排午餐的餐廳，請問他有沒有什麼東西不吃的？ |
| Belinda: No, he is pretty easy, but he does prefer a light lunch. As much as he enjoys Taiwanese food, he would prefer a sandwich and salad for lunch. | 柏琳達：沒有，他還蠻隨和的，但他中午習慣吃清淡一點。雖然他喜歡台菜，可是午餐他還是偏好吃三明治和沙拉。 |

Mark: Right, I think in that case I will book a western restaurant for lunch then. Is there anything else we can pre arrange for him?

馬克：好的，既然這樣的話那我中餐就訂西餐廳，還有什麼其他的事需要先幫他準備的嗎？

Belinda: Yes, he would prefer to stay in a smoking room actually. Would this be a problem?

柏琳達：有，可以麻煩你幫他訂可以抽菸的房間嗎？這會有問題嗎？

Mark: Well, I will check with the hotel, if not, I can find another hotel for him.

馬克：嗯，我來問一下飯店，如果不行的話我就幫他找另一間飯店。

影子跟讀「短對話」

影子跟讀「短段落」

影子跟讀「長段落」

# 訪客的喜好／注意事項－餐廳＋餐點＋房間

▶▶ 「短對話」填空練習 🎧 MP3 026

　　除了前面的「**影子跟讀短對話練習**」，現在試著在聽完對話後，完成下列對話中填空部分，從中強化生活場景中常見的字彙以及拼字能力，答案的話請參照前面的對話喔！

Mark: Hey Belinda, I am making a _____ for _____ for Mr. Moss. Does he have any _____?

馬克：柏琳達您好，我現在要幫摩斯先生安排午餐的餐廳，請問他有沒有什麼東西不吃的？

Belinda: No, he is pretty easy, but he does prefer a _____ lunch. As much as he enjoys _____, he would prefer a _____ and _____ for lunch.

柏琳達：沒有，他還蠻隨和的，但他中午習慣吃清淡一點。雖然他喜歡台菜，可是午餐他還是偏好吃三明治和沙拉。

Mark: Right, I think in that

馬克：好的，既然這樣的

case I will book a _____ for _____ then. Is there anything else we can pre arrange for him?

話那我中餐就訂西餐廳，還有什麼其他的事需要先幫他準備的嗎？

Belinda: Yes, he would prefer to _____ in a _____ _____ actually. Would this be a problem?

柏琳達：有，可以麻煩你幫他訂可以抽菸的房間嗎？這會有問題嗎？

Mark: Well, I will check with the _____, if not, I can find another _____ for him.

馬克：嗯，我來問一下飯店，如果不行的話我就幫他找另一間飯店。

# 與訪客確認行程－行程＋飯店＋日期

▶▶ 影子跟讀「短對話」練習  🎧 MP3 027

此篇為**「影子跟讀短對話練習」**，規劃了由聽**「短對話」**的 shadowing 練習，從最基礎、最易上手的部分切入雅思聽力備考，熟悉各生活場景類的用字，現在就一起動身，開始聽**「短對話」**！

Yvonne: Hi Jimmy, I was wondering if Mr. Harvey's schedule to Taiwan is finalized?

伊凡：吉米您好，我想請問哈維先生的台灣行程都定案了嗎？

Jimmy: More or less, his accommodations are confirmed. He is booked in to stay in Holiday Inn for two nights. The driver will pick him up from the airport the night of 25th, and take him to the hotel. I am just wait-

吉米：差不多了，飯店訂好了，他會在假日飯店住兩晚。司機在 25 號晚上會去接他，然後帶他去飯店。我還在等他其他客戶的確認，看看他們是不是 27 號早上有空，然後我就可以傳一份行程表給

ing to hear back from this other client, to see if they are available in the morning of the 27th, then I will be able to send you the completed schedule.

你。

Yvonne: Sounds good. Thank you so much for your help.

伊凡：太好了！謝謝你的幫忙。

影子跟讀「短對話」

影子跟讀「短段落」

影子跟讀「長段落」

# 與訪客確認行程－
# 行程＋飯店＋日期

▶▶ 「短對話」填空練習 🎧 MP3 027

除了前面的**「影子跟讀短對話練習」**，現在試著在聽完對話後，完成下列對話中填空部分，從中強化生活場景中常見的字彙以及拼字能力，答案的話請參照前面的對話喔！

Yvonne: Hi Jimmy, I was wondering if Mr. Harvey's _____ to Taiwan is finalized?

伊凡：吉米您好，我想請問哈維先生的台灣行程都定案了嗎？

Jimmy: More or less, his _____ are _____. He is booked in to stay in _____ for _____. The _____ will pick him up from the _____ the night of 25th, and take him to the _____. I am just waiting to hear back from

吉米：差不多了，飯店訂好了，他會在假日飯店住兩晚。司機在 25 號晚上會去接他，然後帶他去飯店。我還在等他其他客戶的確認，看看他們是不是 27 號早上有空，然後我就可以傳一份行程表給你。

this other _____, to see if they are available in the _____ of the _____ __, then I will be able to send you the _____.

Yvonne: Sounds _____. Thank you so much for your help.

伊凡：太好了！謝謝你的幫忙。

# 廠商想直接拜訪客戶－行程＋設備＋客戶溝通

▶ 影子跟讀「短對話」練習　🎧 MP3 028

　　此篇為 **「影子跟讀短對話練習」**，規劃了由聽 **「短對話」** 的 shadowing 練習，從最基礎、最易上手的部分切入雅思聽力備考，熟悉各生活場景類的用字，現在就一起動身，開始聽 **「短對話」**！

Kelly: Hi Johnny, I know you are in the process of sorting of the schedule. I was wondering if it's possible to set up a meeting with Tung-Seng company. Mr. Pence would like to do a sales presentation on our latest model.

凱莉：強尼您好，我知道你正為我們的來訪做準備，我是想問你，有沒有機會可以跟東盛公司見個面，因為彭斯先生想跟他們介紹我們最新的設備。

Johnny: Well, I would have to check with Mrs. Lee first. She normally does not in-

強尼：這個嘛，我要先問一下李女士，因為通常她是不會帶廠商去見客戶

volve the supplier directly with our clients.

的。

Kelly: It will be really helpful If you can check with Mrs. Lee. Mr. Pence believes it will be beneficial.

凱莉：好啊，那就麻煩你幫我們跟她溝通一下，因為彭斯先生覺得對商議上會很有幫助。

Johnny: Sure, I will check with her, but I will be honest with you, but it's very unlikely.

強尼：好的，我會幫你問，可是老實說，但是實在是不太可能。

# 廠商想直接拜訪客戶－行程＋設備＋客戶溝通

▶▶ 「短對話」填空練習 🎧 MP3 028

　　除了前面的**「影子跟讀短對話練習」**，現在試著在聽完對話後，完成下列對話中填空部分，從中強化生活場景中常見的字彙以及拼字能力，答案的話請參照前面的對話喔！

Kelly: Hi Johnny, I know you are in the _____ of sorting of the _____. I was wondering if it's possible to set up a meeting with Tung-Seng _____. Mr. Pence would like to do a _____ on our latest _____.

凱莉：強尼您好，我知道你正為我們的來訪做準備，我是想問你，有沒有機會可以跟東盛公司見個面，因為彭斯先生想跟他們介紹我們最新的設備。

Johnny: Well, I would have to check with Mrs. Lee first. She _____ does not involve the _____ direct-

強尼：這個嘛，我要先問一下李女士，因為通常她是不會帶廠商去見客戶的。

ly with our _____.

Kelly: It will be really help-ful If you can _____ with Mrs. Lee. Mr. Pence believes it will be _____.

凱莉：好啊，那就麻煩你幫我們跟她溝通一下，因為彭斯先生覺得對商議上會很有幫助。

Johnny: Sure, I will check with her, but I will be _____ with you, but it's very unlikely.

強尼：好的，我會幫你問，可是老實說，但是實在是不太可能。

# 私人光觀行程－住宿＋房型＋預算

▶ 影子跟讀「短對話」練習 🎧 MP3 029

　　此篇為**「影子跟讀短對話練習」**，規劃了由聽**「短對話」**的 shadowing 練習，從最基礎、最易上手的部分切入雅思聽力備考，熟悉各生活場景類的用字，現在就一起動身，開始聽**「短對話」**！

Yvonne: Thanks for making all the appointments for Mr. Harvey, and there is one more thing. Do you think you can book a couple of nights of accommodation in Kenting for him as well? He would like to stay on for a bit of holiday.

伊凡：謝謝你幫哈維先生安排行程，還有一件事要麻煩你，你可以幫他在墾丁訂兩個晚上的住宿嗎？他想要順便度個假。

Jimmy: Not a problem, what kind of accommodation is he after?

吉米：沒問題，他想要怎樣的房型？

Yvonne: He would prefer to stay in a resort type of accommodation, price range between 150 EURO −200 EURO per night.

伊凡：他喜歡住度假村類型飯店，預算大概是每個晚上 150 到 200 歐元左右。

Jimmy: Sure, there are lots to choose from. I will send you some information and you can let me know which one to book for him.

吉米：好的，那他的選擇還不少，我再傳一些飯店的資料給你，你再跟我說要幫他訂哪一間。

影子跟讀「短對話」

影子跟讀「短段落」

影子跟讀「長段落」

# 私人光觀行程－住宿
# ＋房型＋預算

▶▶ 「短對話」填空練習 🎧 MP3 029

除了前面的**「影子跟讀短對話練習」**，現在試著在聽完對話後，完成下列對話中填空部分，從中強化生活場景中常見的字彙以及拼字能力，答案的話請參照前面的對話喔！

Yvonne: Thanks for making all the _____ for Mr. Harvey, and there is one more thing. Do you think you can _____ a couple of nights of _____ for him as well? He would like to stay on for a bit of _____.

伊凡：謝謝你幫哈維先生安排行程，還有一件事要麻煩你，你可以幫他在墾丁訂兩個晚上的住宿嗎？他想要順便度個假。

Jimmy: Not a problem, what kind of accommodation is he after?

吉米：沒問題，他想要怎樣的房型？

Yvonne: He would prefer to stay in a _____ type of accommodation, _____ between _____ EURO – _____ EURO per night.

伊凡：他喜歡住度假村類型飯店，預算大概是每個晚上 150 到 200 歐元左右。

Jimmy: Sure, there are lots to _____ from. I will send you some _____ and you can let me know which one to book for him.

吉米：好的，那他的選擇還不少，我再傳一些飯店的資料給你，你再跟我說要幫他訂哪一間。

影子跟讀「短對話」

影子跟讀「短段落」

影子跟讀「長段落」

# 詢問工程師行程表－星期＋日期＋月份

▶ 影子跟讀「短對話」練習  🎧 MP3 030

　　此篇為**「影子跟讀短對話練習」**，規劃了由聽「短對話」的 shadowing 練習，從最基礎、最易上手的部分切入雅思聽力備考，熟悉各生活場景類的用字，現在就一起動身，開始聽**「短對話」**！

| | |
|---|---|
| **Peggy:** So do you know which engineers will be coming to do the installation yet? | **佩琪：**那你知道是哪幾個工程師會來安裝了嗎？ |
| **Dexter:** Well, at the moment I got Andrew and Clive available, I know you prefer Mark, but he won't be available until the end of May. I don't think the end user can wait that long. | **戴斯特：**嗯，目前只有安德路還有克萊夫有空，我知道你比較想要馬克去，可是他要到五月底才會有空。我不認為客戶能夠等這麼久。 |

Peggy: Yes, they are in a bit of hurry. I think Andrew and Clive are ok. How soon can they get here?

佩琪：是啊，他們是很急，我覺得安德魯和克萊夫也可以，他們最快什麼時候可以到？

Dexter: Andrew will be finishing his project in Korea at the end of next week. I can arrange for them to arrive in Taipei on 5th of April.

戴斯特：安德魯下星期就會把韓國的案子做完，我可以安排他們四月五日抵達台北。

Peggy: Well, it is a public holiday here. Would you be able to change it to the 6th of April?

佩琪：可是那天是國定假日，不然如果日期改到四月六日如何呢？

影子跟讀「短對話」

影子跟讀「短段落」

影子跟讀「長段落」

# 詢問工程師行程表－星期＋日期＋月份

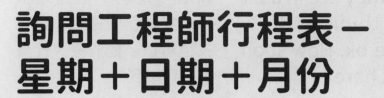

▶▶ 「短對話」填空練習 🎧 MP3 030

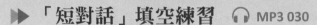

除了前面的**「影子跟讀短對話練習」**，現在試著在聽完對話後，完成下列對話中填空部分，從中強化生活場景中常見的字彙以及拼字能力，答案的話請參照前面的對話喔！

| | |
|---|---|
| Peggy: So do you know which ＿＿＿＿ will be coming to do the ＿＿＿＿ yet? | 佩琪：那你知道是哪幾個工程師會來安裝了嗎？ |
| Dexter: Well, at the moment I got Andrew and Clive ＿＿＿＿, I know you prefer ＿＿＿＿, but he won't be available until the end of ＿＿＿＿. I don't think the ＿＿＿＿ can wait that long. | 戴斯特：嗯，目前只有安德路還有克萊夫有空，我知道你比較想要馬克去，可是他要到五月底才會有空。我不認為客戶能夠等這麼久。 |

Peggy: Yes, they are in a bit of _____. I think Andrew and Clive are ok. How soon can they get here?

佩琪：是啊，他們是很急，我覺得安德魯和克萊夫也可以，他們最快什麼時候可以到？

Dexter: Andrew will be finishing his _____ at the end of next week. I can arrange for them to arrive in _____ on _____.

戴斯特：安德魯下星期就會把韓國的案子做完，我可以安排他們四月五日抵達台北。

Peggy: Well, it is a _____ here. Would you be able to change it to _____?

佩琪：可是那天是國定假日，不然如果日期改到四月六日如何呢？

# 零件延誤－設備＋海關＋零件

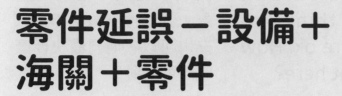

▶▶ 影子跟讀「短對話」練習  🎧 MP3 031

　　此篇為「影子跟讀短對話練習」，規劃了由聽「短對話」的 shadowing 練習，從最基礎、最易上手的部分切入雅思聽力備考，熟悉各生活場景類的用字，現在就一起動身，開始聽「短對話」！

---

Peggy: Did Dexter mention that other than the standard installation, we also need to replace the filter system?

佩琪：戴斯特有跟你提過除了標準的安裝工作之外，還要更換原來的過濾設備嗎？

---

Andrew: Yes, he did.

安德魯：有，他有提到。

---

Peggy: But there is a slight delay with the filter system parts. They got stuck in

佩琪：可是過濾設備的零件有點延誤，目前卡在海關，可能還要好幾天才會

---

customs and will probably take a few more days before they are released to us. Do you think you can start on the installation first and do the filter system later?

發回給我們。你可以先著手開始安裝工作然後晚一點再做過濾設備嗎？

Andrew: I would prefer to do the filter system first, but I guess there is no other way. I just can't sit around and do nothing.

安德魯：我是希望先做過濾設備，可是現在也沒辦法，我總不能在這裡乾等。

Peggy: Phew, thanks for that. I will be in so much trouble if you need those parts right away.

佩琪：喔～你真是救星！如果你堅持要先做過濾設備的話那我就慘了。

影子跟讀「短對話」

影子跟讀「短段落」

影子跟讀「長段落」

139

# 零件延誤－設備＋海關＋零件

▶▶ 「短對話」填空練習　🎧 MP3 031

　　除了前面的**「影子跟讀短對話練習」**，現在試著在聽完對話後，完成下列對話中填空部分，從中強化生活場景中常見的字彙以及拼字能力，答案的話請參照前面的對話喔！

Peggy: Did Dexter _____ __ that other than the _____, we also need to replace the _____?

佩琪：戴斯特有跟你提過除了標準的安裝工作之外，還要更換原來的過濾設備嗎？

Andrew: Yes, he did.

安德魯：有，他有提到。

Peggy: But there is a slight _____ with the filter system parts. They got stuck in _____ and will probably take a few more _____ before they are

佩琪：可是過濾設備的零件有點延誤，目前卡在海關，可能還要好幾天才會發回給我們。你可以先著手開始安裝工作然後晚一點再做過濾設備嗎？

_____ to us. Do you think you can start on the installation first and do the _____ later?

Andrew: I would prefer to do the filter system first, but I guess there is no other way. I just can't _____ __ and do nothing.

安德魯：我是希望先做過濾設備，可是現在也沒辦法，我總不能在這裡乾等。

Peggy: Phew, thanks for that. I will be in so much __ _____ if you need those parts right away.

佩琪：喔～你真是救星！如果你堅持要先做過濾設備的話那我就慘了。

影子跟讀「短對話」

影子跟讀「短段落」

影子跟讀「長段落」

# 對工程師的提點－
# 進度報告＋時程＋零件

▶▶ 影子跟讀「短對話」練習　🎧 MP3 032

此篇為**「影子跟讀短對話練習」**，規劃了由聽**「短對話」**的 shadowing 練習，從最基礎、最易上手的部分切入雅思聽力備考，熟悉各生活場景類的用字，現在就一起動身，開始聽**「短對話」**！

Peggy: Since this is the first time, you work in this factory, there is something you need to know. There is a daily report that you need to fill out at the end of the day and make sure you get the department supervisor to sign it as well.

佩琪：既然這是你第一次到廠房做安裝，有些事情我需要跟你說明。下班前記得要填寫每日施工進度報告，還記得給部門主管簽名。

Andrew: Okay, which one is the department supervisor?

安德魯：好的，那主管是哪一個？

Peggy: It is Mr. Kao. The skinny guy with glasses. He normally does the morning shift and finishes work around 3 pm. The best time to catch him will be around lunch.

佩琪：是高先生，就是那個瘦瘦戴眼鏡的那一個。他通常是輪早班，所以三點就下班了。最容易找到他的時間就是午餐時間。

Andrew: Sure, anything else I need to know?

安德魯：好的，還有什麼是我需要注意的嗎？

Peggy: If you need any small parts, just go to the Maintenance Department. They will be happy to assist you.

佩琪：如果你需要一些小零件，那就直接去找維修部，他們很樂意提供。

影子跟讀「短對話」

影子跟讀「短段落」

影子跟讀「長段落」

# 對工程師的提點－ 進度報告＋時程＋零件

▶▶ 「短對話」填空練習　🎧 MP3 032

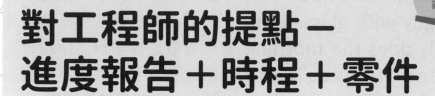

　　除了前面的「影子跟讀短對話練習」，現在試著在聽完對話後，完成下列對話中填空部分，從中強化生活場景中常見的字彙以及拼字能力，答案的話請參照前面的對話喔！

Peggy: Since this is the first time, you work in this ____ _____, there is something you need to know. There is a _____ that you need to _____ at the end of the day and make sure you get the _____ to sign it as well.

佩琪：既然這是你第一次到廠房做安裝，有些事情我需要跟你說明。下班前記得要填寫每日施工進度報告，還記得給部門主管簽名。

Andrew: Okay, which one is the department _____?

安德魯：好的，那主管是哪一個？

Peggy: It is Mr. Kao. The __ _____ guy with _____ __. He _____ does the _____ and finishes work around 3 pm. The best time to _____ him will be around lunch.

佩琪：是高先生，就是那個瘦瘦戴眼鏡的那一個。他通常是輪早班，所以三點就下班了。最容易找到他的時間就是午餐時間。

Andrew: Sure, anything else I need to know?

安德魯：好的，還有什麼是我需要注意的嗎？

Peggy: If you need any ____ _____ parts, just go to the _____. They will be happy to _____ you.

佩琪：如果你需要一些小零件，那就直接去找維修部，他們很樂意提供。

145

# 工程師反應問題－ 訂單＋零件號碼＋庫存

▶▶ 影子跟讀「短對話」練習　🎧 MP3 033

此篇為「影子跟讀短對話練習」，規劃了由聽「短對話」的 shadowing 練習，從最基礎、最易上手的部分切入雅思聽力備考，熟悉各生活場景類的用字，現在就一起動身，開始聽「短對話」！

Andrew: Hello Peggy, I think the client will contact you shortly replacing an order for a set of parts. We are having a problem here. We discovered some of the electrical parts are worn out. We need to replace them; otherwise, it would not work properly.

安德魯：佩琪您好，客戶應該馬上會跟你聯絡要訂一組零件，我們安裝上有些問題，我們發現有些電路零件已經都磨損了，那些一訂要換，不然機器會出問題。

Peggy: Right. Do you have the part numbers? I can

佩琪：好的，那你有零件號碼嗎？我可以查一下有

check whether the parts are in stock. If not, I will put in an urgent order for them.

沒有庫存，如果沒有我就趕快下個緊急訂單。

Andrew: Sure, it is FE104-12 and two other cables. I also had them written down and gave it to the installation supervisor.

安德魯：有，那是 FE104-12 和其他兩組接線，我也有把號碼寫下來，已經拿給安裝負責人了。

Peggy: Thanks for the heads up, I will put the order through once I heard from them.

佩琪：謝謝你先告訴我，他們跟我聯絡之後我會馬上下訂單。

# 工程師反應問題－訂單＋零件號碼＋庫存

▶▶ 「短對話」填空練習  🎧 MP3 033

除了前面的**「影子跟讀短對話練習」**，現在試著在聽完對話後，完成下列對話中填空部分，從中強化生活場景中常見的字彙以及拼字能力，答案的話請參照前面的對話喔！

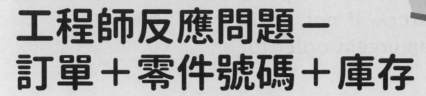

Andrew: Hello Peggy, I think the _____ will __ _____ you shortly replacing an _____ for a set of parts. We are having a problem here. We discovered some of the _____ __ are worn out. We need to replace them; otherwise, it would not work _____ __.

安德魯：佩琪您好，客戶應該馬上會跟你聯絡要訂一組零件，我們安裝上有些問題，我們發現有些電路零件已經都磨損了，那些一訂要換，不然機器會出問題。

Peggy: Right. Do you have the part _____? I can

佩琪：好的，那你有零件號碼嗎？我可以查一下有

check whether the parts are _____. If not, I will put in an _____ for them.

沒有庫存，如果沒有我就趕快下個緊急訂單。

Andrew: Sure, it is _____ _ and two other _____ __. I also had them _____ _ down and gave it to the installation supervisor.

安德魯：有，那是 FE104-12 和其他兩組接線，我也有把號碼寫下來，已經拿給安裝負責人了。

Peggy: Thanks for the heads up, I will put the order through once I heard from them.

佩琪：謝謝你先告訴我，他們跟我聯絡之後我會馬上下訂單。

影子跟讀「短對話」

影子跟讀「短段落」

影子跟讀「長段落」

# 準備試車／驗收－安裝＋測試＋安排

▶▶ 影子跟讀「短對話」練習　🎧 MP3 034

　　此篇為「影子跟讀短對話練習」，規劃了由聽「短對話」的 shadowing 練習，從最基礎、最易上手的部分切入雅思聽力備考，熟悉各生活場景類的用字，現在就一起動身，開始聽「短對話」！

Peggy: Hi Andrew. How is the installation going? Do you think we will be ready for the commissioning?

佩琪：嗨，安德魯，安裝一切都順利嗎？你覺得下禮拜可以準備試車了嗎？

Andrew: The installation is going well, but there is a small hiccup the needs to be fixed with the feeding system. We will do the commissioning in a couple of days, and if all works out, we will be ready for

安德魯：安裝蠻順利的，只是送料系統還有些問題需要調整一下，我們兩天後會先試車，下禮拜就可以正式做驗收測試了。

影子跟讀「短對話」

影子跟讀「短段落」

影子跟讀「長段落」

the final test run next week.

Peggy: That's good to know. Let me know how you go with the test run because Mr. Chou would like to just be there for the final test run. I will organize for him to be there next week if all goes to plan.

佩琪：那太棒了！等試車完畢時麻煩你通知我一下，因為驗收測試的期間周先生想親自到場，如果一切順利的話，我就安排他下星期過去。

# 準備試車／驗收－安裝＋測試＋安排

▶▶ 「短對話」填空練習 🎧 MP3 034

除了前面的**「影子跟讀短對話練習」**，現在試著在聽完對話後，完成下列對話中填空部分，從中強化生活場景中常見的字彙以及拼字能力，答案的話請參照前面的對話喔！

Peggy: Hi Andrew. How is the _____ going? Do you think we will be ready for the _____?

佩琪：嗨，安德魯，安裝一切都順利嗎？你覺得下禮拜可以準備試車了嗎？

Andrew: The installation is going well, but there is a _____ the needs to be _____ with the feeding system. We will do the _____ in a couple of days, and if all works out, we will be ready for the _____ run next week.

安德魯：安裝蠻順利的，只是送料系統還有些問題需要調整一下，我們兩天後會先試車，下禮拜就可以正式做驗收測試了。

Peggy: That's good to know. Let me know how you go with the _____ because Mr. Chou would like to just be there for the final test run. I will _____ __ for him to be there ____ _____ if all goes to _____ __.

佩琪：那太棒了！等試車完畢時麻煩你通知我一下，因為驗收測試的期間周先生想親自到場，如果一切順利的話，我就安排他下星期過去。

影子跟讀「短對話」

影子跟讀「短段落」

影子跟讀「長段落」

# 通知供應廠商已順利完工－文件作業＋證書＋星期

▶ 影子跟讀「短對話」練習 🎧 MP3 035

　　此篇為「影子跟讀短對話練習」，規劃了由聽「短對話」的 shadowing 練習，從最基礎、最易上手的部分切入雅思聽力備考，熟悉各生活場景類的用字，現在就一起動身，開始聽「短對話」！

Peggy: Hi Dexter. Good news for you. The installation is all sorted out and the commissioning and the final acceptance run both went well. We are in the process of getting the paperwork done. The end user will sign the certificate of acceptance shortly.

佩琪：戴斯特您好，有個好消息跟你說，安裝已經完成了，試車還有驗收測試都很順利，我們目前正在處理相關的文件作業，客戶很快就會簽驗收證書了。以離開？他們兩星期後還有其他的安裝工作要做。

Dexter: That's wonderful. So when do you think I can

戴斯特：那太好了，那工程師甚麼時候可以離開？

have the engineers back? They got another project to attend to in two weeks time.

他們兩星期後還有其他的安裝工作要做。

Peggy: Well, they need to stay on for one more week to complete the staff training. If you need them back right after that, then you can arrange for them to fly out either next Friday night or Saturday morning.

佩琪：這樣啊，他們還需要多留一個星期來做員工訓練，如果你很急著要他們回去，那就安排下星期五晚上或是星期六早上回去好了。

# 通知供應廠商已順利完工－文件作業＋證書＋星期

▶▶「短對話」填空練習 🎧 MP3 035

除了前面的**「影子跟讀短對話練習」**，現在試著在聽完對話後，完成下列對話中填空部分，從中強化生活場景中常見的字彙以及拼字能力，答案的話請參照前面的對話喔！

Peggy: Hi Dexter. Good news for you. The installation is all sorted out and the commissioning and the _____ run both went well. We are in the _____ of getting the _____ done. The end user will __ _____ the _____ of _____ shortly.

佩琪：戴斯特您好，有個好消息跟你說，安裝已經完成了，試車還有驗收測試都很順利，我們目前正在處理相關的文件作業，客戶很快就會簽驗收證書了。以離開？他們兩星期後還有其他的安裝工作要做。

Dexter: That's _____. So when do you think I can have the _____ back?

戴斯特：那太好了，那工程師甚麼時候可以離開？他們兩星期後還有其他的

They got another _____ __ to attend to in _____ time.

安裝工作要做。

Peggy: Well, they need to stay on for one more week to _____ the _____ __. If you need them back right after that, then you can _____ for them to fly out either _____ night or _____.

佩琪：這樣啊，他們還需要多留一個星期來做員工訓練，如果你很急著要他們回去，那就安排下星期五晚上或是星期六早上回去好了。

# 常考高階名詞－Captain America美國隊長 ❶

▶▶ 影子跟讀「短段落」練習 🎧 MP3 036

　　此篇為**「影子跟讀短段落練習」**，規劃了由聽**「短段落」**的 shadowing 練習，強化考生定位和聆聽數個句子的專注力，聽 section 3 和 section 4 都覺得瞬間變得簡單，現在就一起動身，開始聽**「短段落」**！

　　Steve Rogers was born in New York City in the 1920s. Even though he wanted to contribute to the World War II, he was rejected for the military recruitments for multiple times due to his health and physical problems. Even so, his enthusiasm never dropped. He again attempted to enlist during an exhibition of future technologies.

　　史蒂夫‧羅傑斯出生於 1920 年代的紐約市。雖然他想在二次世界大戰中有所貢獻，但是由於他的健康和體格的問題，他卻被軍事招聘多次的拒絕。即便如此。他熱情不懈。他再次在一個未來技術展覽期間嘗試應徵。

　　Dr. Abraham Erskine overheard Roger's conversation and decided to put him into the Strategic Scientific Reserve and part of the super-solder experiment. In this team, Rogers later gained his position as the chosen one with his intelligence and bravery.

亞伯拉罕・厄斯金博士在聽到羅傑的對話後，決定把他送上科學戰略儲備團隊並成為超級戰士實驗的一部分。在這個團隊中，羅傑斯後來因為他的智慧與勇氣，成為了雀屏中選的那一位。

Erskine gave Rogers the super soldier treatment. He was injected with a special serum and dosed with "vita-rays" which made him taller and more muscular. From his attributes, such as endurance, agility, durability, and healing power, Rogers has a near superman power. Also, with the super-soldier serum regained ability, Rogers' abilities do not wear off over time. Erskine was then killed by one of Schmidt's assassins, Heinz Kruger, who later on committed suicide.

厄斯金給了羅傑斯超級戰士的療程。他被注射一種特殊含有「VITA-射線」劑量的血清，這使他的身高和肌肉更為發達。從他的特質，像是耐力、敏捷度、耐久性及自癒能力，羅傑斯有著近超人的能力。另外有著超級戰士血清補給能力，羅傑斯的能力從不會減弱。厄斯金爾後被施密特的一名刺客亨氏克魯格刺殺身亡，亨氏克魯格後來也自殺了。

此部分為「**影子跟讀短段落練習❷**」，請重新播放音檔並完成試題，現在就一起動身，開始完成「**短段落練習❷**」吧！

Steve Rogers was born in 1.＿＿＿＿＿＿ in the 1920s. He was rejected for the 2.＿＿＿＿＿ for multiple times due to his 3.＿＿＿＿＿ and 4.＿＿＿＿＿ problems. Even so, his 5.＿＿＿＿＿ never dropped. He again attempted to enlist during an 6.＿＿＿＿＿ of future technologies. Dr. Abraham Erskine overheard Roger's 7.＿＿＿＿＿ and decided to put him into the Strategic 8.＿＿＿＿＿ and part of the super-solder 9.＿＿＿＿＿. In this team, Rogers later on gained his 10.＿＿＿＿＿ as the chosen one with his intelligence and bravery.

Erskine gave Rogers the super soldier 11.＿＿＿＿＿. He was injected with a 12.＿＿＿＿＿ and dosed with "vita-rays" which made him taller and more 13.＿＿＿＿＿. From his 14.＿＿＿＿＿, such as 15.＿＿＿＿＿, agility, 16.＿＿＿＿＿, and healing power, Rogers has a near superman power. Erskine was then killed by one of Schmidt's 17.＿＿＿＿＿, Heinz Kruger, who later on committed 18.＿＿＿＿＿.

## ▶▶ 參考答案

| | |
|---|---|
| 1. New York City | 2. military recruitments |
| 3. health | 4. physical |
| 5. enthusiasm | 6. exhibition |
| 7. conversation | 8. Scientific Reserve |
| 9. experiment | 10. position |
| 11. treatment | 12. special serum |
| 13. muscular | 14. attributes |
| 15. endurance | 16. durability |
| 17. assassins | 18. suicide |

影子跟讀「短對話」

影子跟讀「短段落」

影子跟讀「長段落」

# 文件作業＋證書＋星期＝ Captain America美國隊長 ❷

▶▶ 影子跟讀「短段落」練習 🎧 MP3 037

　　此篇為「影子跟讀短段落練習」，規劃了由聽「短段落」的 shadowing 練習，強化考生定位和聆聽數個句子的專注力，聽 section 3 和 section 4 都覺得瞬間變得簡單，現在就一起動身，開始聽「短段落」！

　　For a long time, Rogers was touring the nation in a colorful costume as "Captain America" to promote war bonds. During his tour of Italy, Rogers learned that his good friend Barnes might be killed by Schmidt's forces. He refused to believe that his friend was dead, and insisted to mount a solo rescue. Rogers infiltrated the fortress of Schmidt's Hydra organization and freed Barnes and many other prisoners.

　　有很長一段時間，羅傑斯身穿五顏六色的「美國隊長」制服在各地販賣戰爭債券。他在義大利旅遊的期間，羅傑斯得知他的好朋友巴恩斯可能被施密特的部隊給殺了。他拒絕相信他的朋友死了，堅持要安排一個單獨的救援行動。羅傑斯滲透進施密特九頭蛇組織的堡壘，並釋放巴恩斯和許多其他的囚犯。

Rogers then was given the advanced outfit and equipment, most notably a circular shield made of vibranium, a rare, nearly indestructible metal. Rogers often uses his shield as an offensive throwing weapon. Combining his skills with his shield, he can attack multiple targets in succession with a single throw or even cause a boomerang-like return from a throw to attack an enemy from behind. Rogers and his team later on started an attack to stop Schmidt from using weapons of mass destruction on all major cities across the globe. Rogers successfully stopped Schmidt's evil.

之後，羅傑斯被賦予了先進的服裝和設備，最值得注意的是用振金所做的圓形盾牌。這是非常難得可見，幾乎堅不可摧的金屬。羅傑斯經常用他的盾牌作為進攻的投擲武器。結合他的技能和他的盾牌，他可以利用單擲連續攻擊多個目標，甚至以迴旋方式從背後攻擊敵人。羅傑斯和他的團隊後來就開始攻擊在世界各主要城市使用大規模殺傷性武器的施密特。羅傑斯成功阻止了施密特的邪惡

影子跟讀「短對話」

影子跟讀「短段落」

影子跟讀「長段落」

此部分為「**影子跟讀短段落練習❷**」，請重新播放音檔並完成試題，現在就一起動身，開始完成「**短段落練習❷**」吧！

For a long time, Rogers was touring the nation in a 1._____ as "Captain America" to promote war 2._____. During his tour of 3._____, Rogers learned that his good friend Barnes might be killed by Schmidt's forces. He refused to believe that his 4._____ was dead, and insisted to mount a 5._____. Rogers infiltrated the 6._____ of Schmidt's Hydra organization and freed Barnes and many other 7._____.

Rogers then was given the advanced outfit and 8._____, most notably a circular 9._____ made of vibranium, a rare, nearly indestructible 10._____. Rogers often uses his shield as an offensive 11._____. Combining his skills with his shield, he can attack multiple targets in succession with a single throw or even cause a boomerang-like return from a throw to attack an 12._____ from behind. Rogers and his 13._____ later on started an attack to stop Schmidt from using weapons of mass 14._____ on all 15._____ across the globe. Rogers 16._____ stopped Schmidt's evil.

## ▶▶ 參考答案

| | |
|---|---|
| 1. colorful costume | 2. bonds |
| 3. Italy | 4. friend |
| 5. solo rescue | 6. fortress |
| 7. prisoners | 8. equipment |
| 9. shield | 10. metal |
| 11. throwing weapon | 12. enemy |
| 13. team | 14. destruction |
| 15. major cities | 16. successfully |

影子跟讀「短對話」

影子跟讀「短段落」

影子跟讀「長段落」

# 國名＋常考名詞－
# The Red Skull紅骷髏

▶▶ **影子跟讀「短段落」練習** 🎧 MP3 038

此篇為**「影子跟讀短段落練習」**，規劃了由聽**「短段落」**的 shadowing 練習，強化考生定位和聆聽數個句子的專注力，聽 **section 3** 和 **section 4** 都覺得瞬間變得簡單，現在就一起動身，開始聽**「短段落」**！

Like most devils, Johann Schmidt had a tragic childhood. Hanging around with the wrong person during his upbringing eventually pushed him to the dark path. Johann was born in a small village in Germany. His mother dies from giving birth to him which drove his drunken father to drown the infant Johann. Saved by the delivering doctor, Johann's father eventually committed suicide, and Johann was forced into an orphanage.

如同許多惡棍，約翰施密特有一個悲慘的童年。成長過程中與錯的人相伴最終將他推向黑暗的道路。約翰出生在德國的一個小村莊。他的母親在生下他後便死亡，因此他酗酒的父親企圖淹死嬰兒約翰。約翰被接生的醫生救起後，他的父親最終自殺了。約翰被迫住進一所孤兒院。

During his upbringing, he got bullied all the time. Thus, he developed an antisocial personality and slowly began to think that every man was his enemy. Johann eventually ran away from the orphanage and started his life on the streets. His first murder killed a Jewish girl with a shovel, a girl he liked but rejected him.

在他的成長過程中，他總是受到霸凌。因此他發展出了反社會人格，慢慢開始認為每個人都是他的敵人。約翰最終還是從孤兒院逃離，並開始在大街上生活。他第一次殺人是用鏟子殺死了一個他喜歡卻拒絕他的猶太女孩。

After years of shady work below Hitler, Johann proudly became an S.S. Officer. Later on, he was trained personally by the Fuhrer of Germany to fit Hitler's requirement, becoming the 2nd most powerful man in Germany. He killed his former officer who failed to train him under Hitler's ideals for S.S. Officer.

多年來在納粹下做黑幕的工作，約翰自豪地成為 S.S.官。後來，他被德國的元首親自培訓，以適應希特勒的要求，成了德國境內第二個最有權勢的人。他殺死了之前沒有成功栽培自己成為希特勒理想 S.S 官員的前任長官。

影子跟讀「短對話」

影子跟讀「短段落」

影子跟讀「長段落」

此部分為「影子跟讀短段落練習❷」，請重新播放音檔並完成試題，現在就一起動身，開始完成「**短段落練習❷**」吧！

Like most devils, Johann Schmidt had a 1.＿＿＿＿＿＿＿. Hanging around with the wrong person during his 2.＿＿＿＿＿ ＿＿＿＿ eventually pushed him to the 3.＿＿＿＿＿＿. Johann was born in a 4.＿＿＿＿＿＿ in 5.＿＿＿＿＿＿. His mother dies from giving 6.＿＿＿＿＿＿ to him which drove his 7.＿＿＿＿＿ father to drown the 8.＿＿＿＿＿＿ Johann. Saved by the 9.＿＿＿＿＿＿, Johann's father eventually committed 10.＿＿＿＿＿＿, and Johann was forced into an 11.＿＿＿＿＿＿.

During his upbringing, he got bullied all the time. Thus, he developed an 12.＿＿＿＿＿＿ and started his life on the streets. His first murder killed a 13.＿＿＿＿＿＿ with a 14.＿＿＿＿＿＿, a girl he liked but rejected him.

After years of shady work below Hitler, Johann proudly became an S.S. Officer. Later on, he was trained personally by the Fuhrer of Germany to fit Hitler's 15.＿＿＿＿＿＿, becoming the 2nd most powerful man in Germany. He killed his former officer who failed to train him under Hitler's 16.＿＿＿＿＿＿ for S.S. Officer.

# ▶▶ 參考答案

1. tragic childhood
2. upbringing
3. dark path
4. small village
5. Germany
6. birth
7. drunken
8. infant
9. delivering doctor
10. suicide
11. orphanage
12. antisocial personality
13. Jewish girl
14. shovel
15. requirement
16. ideals

影子跟讀「短對話」

影子跟讀「短段落」

影子跟讀「長段落」

# 數字＋常考名詞－ Spiderman 蜘蛛人 ❶

▶▶ 影子跟讀「短段落」練習 🎧 MP3 039

　　此篇為「影子跟讀短段落練習」，規劃了由聽「短段落」的 shadowing 練習，強化考生定位和聆聽數個句子的專注力，聽 section 3 和 section 4 都覺得瞬間變得簡單，現在就一起動身，開始聽「短段落」！

　　Both his parents were killed in a plane crash, so Peter Parker was raised by his uncle Ben and aunt May in Forest Hills, Queens, New York. During his high school years, even though he was known as a science whiz, he was extremely shy and was targeted by his peers.

　　父母都在一次飛機失事中喪生，所以彼得・帕克是由他的班叔叔和梅阿姨在皇后區的森林山所扶養長大。在他高中時，儘管他被公認是一個科學奇才，他非常害羞，而且是同儕欺侮的目標。

　　When he was 15 years old, he attended a public science exhibition and was bitten on the hand by a radioactive spider. Instead of getting ill from the poison,

Parker magically gained the ability to adhere to walls and ceilings. He also acquired the agility and proportionate strength just like a spider. As a science genius, he then developed a gadget that allows him to fire adhesive webbing through wrist-mounted barrels. As a shy boy, as much as he wanted to capitalize on his new abilities, he was too afraid to use his own identity. Therefore, he developed the Spiderman costume and became a novel TV star.

　　在他 15 歲時，他參加一個公開的科學展覽，並被放射性的蜘蛛咬傷了手。非但沒有因為毒藥而生病，帕克神奇獲得了爬牆壁和天花板的能力。他還獲得了敏捷性和相稱性，就跟一個蜘蛛一樣。作為一門科學天才，他隨後開發出一個小工具，讓他可以藉由腕帶式的機具發射有黏性的蜘蛛網。作為一個害羞的少年，雖然他希望可以利用他新的能力，但他非常害怕使用自己的身份。因此，他開發出了蜘蛛人的服裝，並成為一個新奇的電視明星。

影子跟讀「短對話」

影子跟讀「短段落」

影子跟讀「長段落」

## ▶▶▶ 影子跟讀「短段落」練習 🎧 MP3 039

　　此部分為「**影子跟讀短段落練習❷**」，請重新播放音檔並完成試題，現在就一起動身，開始完成「**短段落練習❷**」吧！

　　Both his parents were killed in a 1.＿＿＿＿＿＿＿, so Peter Parker was raised by his uncle Ben and aunt May in Forest Hills, Queens, New York. During his high school years, even though he was known as a 2.＿＿＿＿＿＿, he was extremely shy and was 3.＿＿＿＿＿＿ by his 4.＿＿＿＿＿＿.

　　When he was 5.＿＿＿＿＿＿ years old, he attended a public science 6.＿＿＿＿＿＿ and was bitten on the 7.＿＿＿＿＿＿ by a 8.＿＿＿＿＿＿. Instead of getting ill from the poison, Parker magically gained the ability to adhere to walls and 9.＿＿＿＿＿＿. He also acquired the 10.＿＿＿＿＿＿ and proportionate strength just like a spider. As a science 11.＿＿＿＿＿＿, he then developed a 12.＿＿＿＿＿＿ that allows him to fire adhesive webbing through wrist-mounted 13.＿＿＿＿＿＿. As a 14.＿＿＿＿＿＿ boy, as much as he wanted to 15.＿＿＿＿＿＿ on his new abilities, he was too afraid to use his own 16.＿＿＿＿＿＿. Therefore, he developed the Spiderman 17.＿＿＿＿＿＿ and became a 18.＿＿＿＿＿＿.

## ▶▶ 參考答案

| | |
|---|---|
| 1. plane crash | 2. science whiz |
| 3. targeted | 4. peers |
| 5. 15 | 6. exhibition |
| 7. hand | 8. radioactive spider |
| 9. ceilings | 10. agility |
| 11. genius | 12. gadget |
| 13. barrels | 14. shy |
| 15. capitalize | 16. identity |
| 17. costume | 18. novel TV star |

影子跟讀「短對話」

影子跟讀「短段落」

影子跟讀「長段落」

# 國名＋常考名詞＋學校－ Spiderman 蜘蛛人 ❷

▶▶ 影子跟讀「短段落」練習　🎧 MP3 040

　　此篇為「影子跟讀短段落練習」，規劃了由聽「短段落」的 shadowing 練習，強化考生定位和聆聽數個句子的專注力，聽 section 3 和 section 4 都覺得瞬間變得簡單，現在就一起動身，開始聽「短段落」！

　　Different from other superheroes like Batman or Superman who are handsome or rich, Spiderman lived with his aunt May in a tiny apartment in New York and was struggling to make a living, even to pay the rent. Due to his lonely and bullied teenage life, Parker got used to ignoring any incidents that happened close to him. Because of that, he missed the chance to stop a fleeing thief who robbed and killed his dearly beloved uncle Ben. Parker regretted that he didn't pay enough attention to his surroundings and society. Then, the principle which his uncle had taught him - "With great power there must also come – greater responsibility！" was a huge awakening to him.

影子跟讀「短對話」

影子跟讀「短段落」

影子跟讀「長段落」

　　與蝙蝠俠、超人等可能帥氣或富有的其他超級英雄不同，蜘蛛人與他的阿姨住在紐約的一個小公寓，努力謀生，甚至連交房租都很掙扎。由於他孤獨且被欺負的青少年生活，帕克習慣性的忽略任何發生在他身邊的事件。正因為如此，他錯過了可以阻止搶劫並殺害他最親愛班叔叔的小偷的機會。帕克對於自己不夠重視周圍環境及社會這件事感到遺憾。於是，他叔叔教他的原則－「強大力量後跟隨而來的是一更重大的責任！」使他有很大的覺醒。

He enrolled at Empire State University after high school where he met his best friend Harry Osborn and his girlfriend Gwen Stacy. The tragedy started there. Gwen's father, George Stacy, an NYPD police officer was accidentally killed during a fight between Spiderman and Doctor Octopus. Gwen blamed Spiderman for the death for years but eventually forgave him. Harry Osborn's father, Norman Osborn, was the founder of Oscorp, an organization known for supplying weapons to the military.

　　高中畢業後，他就讀於帝國州立大學，並認識了他最好的朋友哈利・奧斯本和他的女友格溫・史黛西。這正是悲劇的開始。格溫的父親，喬治・史黛西，一個紐約市的警察在蜘蛛人和章魚博士鬥爭之中不幸喪生。格溫多年來指責蜘蛛人，但最終還是原諒了他。哈利・奧斯本的父親，諾曼・奧斯本，是 Oscorp 的創始人。Oscorp 是著名的軍事武器供應商。

## ▶▶▶ 影子跟讀「短段落」練習　🎧 MP3 040

　　此部分為「影子跟讀短段落練習❷」，請重新播放音檔並完成試題，現在就一起動身，開始完成「短段落練習❷」吧！

　　Different from other superheroes like Batman or Superman who are 1._____ or rich, Spiderman lived with his 2._____ May in a tiny 3._____ in 4._____ and was struggling to make a living, even to pay the 5._____. Due to his lonely and bullied 6._____ life, Parker got used to ignoring any incidents that happened close to him. Because of that, he missed the chance to stop a fleeing 7._____ who robbed and killed his dearly 8._____ Ben. Parker regretted that he didn't pay enough attention to his 9._____ and society. Then, the 10._____ which his uncle had taught him - "With great power there must also come – greater responsibility！" was a huge 11._____ to him.

　　He enrolled at Empire State 12._____ after high school where he met his best friend Harry Osborn and his girlfriend Gwen Stacy. The 13._____ started there. Gwen's father, George Stacy, an NYPD 14._____ was accidentally killed during a fight between Spiderman n and Doctor Octopus. Gwen blamed Spiderman for the 15._____ for years but eventually forgave him. Harry Osborn's father, Norman Osborn, was the founder of Oscorp,

an 16.＿＿＿＿＿＿ known for 17.＿＿＿＿＿＿ weapons
to the 18.＿＿＿＿＿＿.

## ▶▶ 參考答案

| | |
|---|---|
| 1. handsome | 2. aunt |
| 3. apartment | 4. New York |
| 5. rent | 6. teenage |
| 7. thief | 8. beloved uncle |
| 9. surroundings | 10. principle |
| 11. awakening | 12. University |
| 13. tragedy | 14. police officer |
| 15. death | 16. organization |
| 17. supplying | 18. military |

# 橋＋顏色＋常考名詞－ The Green Goblin綠惡魔

▶▶ 影子跟讀「短段落」練習　🎧 MP3 041

　　此篇為「影子跟讀短段落練習」，規劃了由聽「短段落」的 shadowing 練習，強化考生定位和聆聽數個句子的專注力，聽 section 3 和 section 4 都覺得瞬間變得簡單，現在就一起動身，開始聽「短段落」！

　　After gaining the full power to control Oscorp, Norman once discovered that Stromm had developed a strength and intelligence enhancement formula, but it was still experimental. Norman did not care. He attempted to create the formula, but the formula turned green and exploded in his face. The formula indeed increased his intelligence and strength, but the side effect was that it led him to destructive insanity.

　　在獲得 Oscorp 的完全掌控權後，諾曼有一次發現史湯姆開發了一種可以提升力量及智慧的配方，雖然這個配方仍是實驗性的。諾曼並不在意。他試圖創造這個配方，但配方變為了綠色，並在他的臉上爆炸。這個配方確實增加了他的智慧和力量，但副作用是它導致了他精神錯亂。

Norman Osborn then created his secret identity as the Green Goblin. What he did was become the boss who organizes all the crimes in the city. His desire to enlarge his business and the insanity he got from the formula led him down the road of no return. Norman first intended to cement his position by having a partnership with Spiderman, but it was unsuccessful. He then held a great grudge against Spiderman. Eventually, he found out that Spiderman was his son's best friend, Peter Parker. In order to get back at Spiderman for refusing to work with him, the Green Goblin kidnapped Parker's girlfriend, Gwen Stacy, and pushed her off the Brooklyn Bridge. Spiderman couldn't help but go for revenge.

諾曼‧奧斯本爾後創造了他的秘密身份—綠惡魔。他組織全市的罪犯，並成為他們的主腦。他的目的是擴大他的事業。而他從配方所得到的精神錯亂導致他的不歸路。諾曼本想利用與蜘蛛人合作來鞏固他的地位，但並不成功。他因此非常怨恨蜘蛛人。最終，他發現了蜘蛛人是他兒子最好的朋友，彼得‧ 帕克。為了報復蜘蛛人拒絕與他合作，綠惡魔綁架了帕克的女友格溫‧史黛西，並把她丟下布魯克林大橋。蜘蛛人忍無可忍決定報復。

此部分為「影子跟讀短段落練習❷」，請重新播放音檔並完成試題，現在就一起動身，開始完成「短段落練習❷」吧！

After gaining the full power to control Oscorp, Norman once discovered that Stromm had developed a 1._____ and intelligence enhancement 2._____, but it was still 3._____. Norman did not care. He attempted to create the formula, but the formula turned 4._____ and exploded in his face. The formula indeed increased his intelligence and strength, but the 5._____ was that it led him to 6._____.

Norman Osborn then created his 7._____ as the Green Goblin. What he did was become 8._____ who organizes all the crimes in the city. His desire to 9._____ his business and the insanity he got from the formula led him down the road of no return. Norman first intended to cement his 10._____ by having a 11._____ with Spiderman, but it was 12._____. He then held a great grudge against Spiderman. Eventually, he found out that Spiderman was his son's 13._____, Peter Parker. In order to get back at Spiderman for refusing to work with him, the Green Goblin kidnapped Parker's 14._____, Gwen Stacy, and pushed her off the 15.__

_____. Spiderman couldn't help but go for 16._____
_____.

## ▶▶ 參考答案

| | |
|---|---|
| 1. strength | 2. formula |
| 3. experimental | 4. green |
| 5. side effect | 6. destructive insanity |
| 7. secret identity | 8. the boss |
| 9. enlarge | 10. position |
| 11. partnership | 12. unsuccessful |
| 13. best friend | 14. girlfriend |
| 15. Brooklyn Bridge | 16. revenge |

# 內科醫生＋常考名詞和形容詞－Batman蝙蝠俠 **1**

▶▶ 影子跟讀「短段落」練習  🎧 MP3 042

　　此篇為**「影子跟讀短段落練習」**，規劃了由聽**「短段落」**的 shadowing 練習，強化考生定位和聆聽數個句子的專注力，聽 section 3 和 section 4 都覺得瞬間變得簡單，現在就一起動身，開始聽**「短段落」**！

　　Bruce Wayne was born into a wealthy family in Gotham City. When he was a kid, he witnessed his parents, the physician Dr.Thomas Wayne and his wife Martha Wayne, getting murdered by a mugger with a gun in front of his very eyes. He was traumatized but swore revenge in all criminals. Growing up, he became a successful business magnate. He was an American billionaire and owned the Wayne Enterprises. In his everyday identity, he acted like a playboy, a heavy drinker, just like many other wealthy men.

　　布魯斯・韋恩出生在高譚市一個富裕的家庭。當他還是個孩子時，他眼睜睜的看著他的父母，托馬斯・韋恩博士和他的妻子瑪莎・韋恩，被一個搶劫犯槍殺身亡。他受到創傷，但誓言對罪

犯復仇。長大後，他成為了一個成功的商業鉅子。他是美國的一個億萬富翁，並擁有韋恩企業。他日常的身份，就像一個花花公子，天天喝酒，就與許多其他有錢的男人一樣。

But in reality, he did his best maintaining his physical fitness and mental acuity. He also developed a bat inspired persona to fight crime. Dressing up as Batman, Wayne kept the city safe and fought against crimes for most of his night life.

但在現實中，他保持最好的體能和敏銳的智能。他也開發了一個由蝙蝠作為啟發的人物來打擊犯罪。裝扮成蝙蝠俠，韋恩在他大部分的夜生活時保持城市的安全及打擊犯罪。

Batman does not possess any superpowers. He relies on his genius intellect, physical prowess, martial arts abilities, detective skills, science and technology, vast wealth, and an indomitable will. Even Superman considers Batman to be one of the most brilliant human beings on the planet.

蝙蝠俠沒有任何超能力。他依靠他天生的智慧、高強的體能、精湛的武藝、偵探的技能、科學與技術、巨大的財富和不屈不撓的意志。即便是超人都認為蝙蝠俠是這個星球上最聰明的人類之一。

影子跟讀「短對話」

影子跟讀「短段落」

影子跟讀「長段落」

## ▶▶▶ 影子跟讀「短段落」練習 🎧 MP3 042

此部分為「**影子跟讀短段落練習❷**」，請重新播放音檔並完成
試題，現在就一起動身，開始完成「**短段落練習❷**」吧！

Bruce Wayne was born into a 1.＿＿＿＿＿＿ in Gotham City. When he was a 2.＿＿＿＿＿＿, he witnessed his
parents, the 3.＿＿＿＿＿＿ Dr. Thomas Wayne and his
wife Martha Wayne, getting murdered by a 4.＿＿＿＿＿＿
with a gun in front of his very eyes. He was traumatized but
swore 5.＿＿＿＿＿＿ in all criminals. Growing up, he became a successful 6.＿＿＿＿＿＿. He was an American 7.＿
＿＿＿＿＿＿ and owned the Wayne Enterprises. In his everyday 8.＿＿＿＿＿＿, he acted like a 9.＿＿＿＿＿＿, a
heavy drinker, just like many other wealthy men.

But in reality, he did his best maintaining his 10.＿＿＿
＿＿＿ and mental 11.＿＿＿＿＿＿. He also developed a
bat inspired 12.＿＿＿＿＿＿ to fight crime. Batman does
not possess any superpowers. He relies on his 13.＿＿＿＿
＿＿ intellect, physical prowess, martial arts abilities, 14.＿＿
＿＿＿＿＿ skills, science and technology, vast wealth, and an
15.＿＿＿＿＿＿. Even Superman considers Batman to be
one of the most 16.＿＿＿＿＿＿ human beings on the
planet.

## ▶▶ 參考答案

| | |
|---|---|
| 1. wealthy family | 2. kid |
| 3. physician | 4. mugger |
| 5. revenge | 6. business magnate |
| 7. billionaire | 8. identity |
| 9. playboy | 10. physical fitness |
| 11. acuity | 12. persona |
| 13. genius | 14. detective |
| 15. indomitable will | 16. brilliant |

# 城市＋設備＋常考名詞－Batman蝙蝠俠 ❷

▶▶ 影子跟讀「短段落」練習 🎧 MP3 043

此篇為「影子跟讀短段落練習」，規劃了由聽「短段落」的 shadowing 練習，強化考生定位和聆聽數個句子的專注力，聽 section 3 和 section 4 都覺得瞬間變得簡單，現在就一起動身，開始聽「短段落」！

One of the reasons why he trains himself to become one of the best fighters is that he refuses to use guns during battles since it is the weapon that killed his parents.He travels around the world to acquire the skills needed to bring criminals to justice.

他將自己訓練成為最好的戰鬥武器之一的原因，是因為他在戰鬥過程中拒絕使用的槍枝，因為它是殺害其父母的武器。他周遊世界各地取得技能，讓他可以將罪犯繩之以法。

Besides mental and physical training, Wayne's inexhaustible wealth allows him access to the greatest and most advanced technology, furthermore building the overall top gadgets. Starting with Batmobile, the primary vehicle of Batman, it is not only a "car". It is a self-powered, transformable fighting motor vehicle. He also owns a "Utility belt" which keeps most of his field equipment, the crime-fighting tools, weapons, and investigative instruments besides guns.

除了心理和體能訓練之外，韋恩取之不盡、用之不竭的財富讓他可以利用最好，也最先進的科技來構建最好的工具。從蝙蝠車開始，這是蝙蝠俠的主要交通工具。它不僅是一輛「車」，它自發供電，並可轉換成戰鬥摩托車。他還擁有一個「功能腰帶」，這個腰帶裡放置了他大部分在打擊犯罪的工具、武器和調查儀器，除了槍枝以外。

In order to let all the people in need to get in touch with him when needed, he also set up a whole bunch of Bat-Signals on top of buildings. When he sees the bat symbol from anywhere in Gotham City, he knows his mission is on. He also gets supports from his butler Alfred, commissioner Jim Gordon, and vigilante allies such as Robin.

並且為了讓所有需要他的人能與他取得聯繫，他還在建築物頂端設立了一大堆蝙蝠信號。當他在任何地方看到在高譚市裡的蝙蝠象徵，他便知道那是他的使命。他也從他的管家阿爾弗雷德，專員戈登・吉姆和維持治安的盟友，如羅賓那裡得到支持。

影子跟讀「短對話」

影子跟讀「短段落」

影子跟讀「長段落」

*187*

此部分為「**影子跟讀短段落練習❷**」，請重新播放音檔並完成試題，現在就一起動身，開始完成「**短段落練習❷**」吧！

One of the reasons why he trains himself to become one of the best 1._____ is that he refuses to use 2._____ during battles since it is the weapon that killed his 3._____. He travels around the world to acquire the skills needed to bring 4._____ to justice. Besides mental and 5._____, Wayne's 6._____ allows him access to the greatest and most 7._____, furthermore building the overall top 8._____. Starting with Batmobile, the 9._____ of Batman, it is not only a "car". He also owns a "Utility belt" which keeps most of his field 10._____, the crime-fighting tools, weapons, and investigative 11._____ besides guns.

In order to let all the people in need to get in touch with him when needed, he also set up a whole bunch of Bat-Signals on top of 12._____. When he sees the bat 13._____ from anywhere in Gotham 14._____, he knows his 15._____ is on. He also gets supports from his butler Alfred, 16._____ Jim Gordon, and vigilante allies such as Robin.

## ▶▶ 參考答案

| | |
|---|---|
| 1. fighters | 2. guns |
| 3. parents | 4. criminals |
| 5. physical training | 6. inexhaustible wealth |
| 7. advanced technology | 8. gadgets |
| 9. primary vehicle | 10. equipment |
| 11. instruments | 12. buildings |
| 13. symbol | 14. City |
| 15. mission | 16. commissioner |

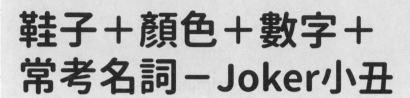

# 鞋子＋顏色＋數字＋常考名詞－Joker小丑

▶▶ **影子跟讀「短段落」練習** 🎧 MP3 044

　　此篇為**「影子跟讀短段落練習」**，規劃了由聽**「短段落」**的 shadowing 練習，強化考生定位和聆聽數個句子的專注力，聽 section 3 和 section 4 都覺得瞬間變得簡單，現在就一起動身，開始聽**「短段落」**！

　　No one really knows where this bleached white skin, red lips, and green hair joker actually came from. There is one indication that says that the Joker quitted his job to become a stand-up comedian to support his wife. Economic conditions led to his agreement with a robbery. Although the robbery was successful, the Joker fell into a giant chemical vat when he attempted to escape from Batman. The chemical inside the vat changed the whole look of Joker. Even worse, the Joker found out that both his wife and unborn child were dead due to an accident.

　　沒有人真正知道這個皮膚漂到白皙、紅潤的嘴唇、綠色的頭髮的小丑實際上是從哪裡來的。有一個說法是，小丑辭去了工

作，成為一個丑角來支持他的妻子。但實際上沒有那麼順利，經濟狀況使他同意了幫忙搶劫。搶劫雖然成功，但小丑在他試圖從蝙蝠俠那裡逃脫時，掉進了一個化學大桶。甕內的化學藥劑改變小丑的整個外觀。更糟的是，小丑發現，他的妻子和未出生的孩子在一場意外中身亡。

The Joker went insane and became the evil Joker that we know today. He also put the blame on Batman. Every crime The Joker does is to get Batman's attention. From murder, theft to terrorism, nothing scares the man in the purple suite with a long-tailed jacket, the string tie, the striped pants, and the pointed-toe shoes. He once claimed that he killed more than 2000 people. Joker is an extreme psychopath that thinks everything he does is funny and humorous. However, they are only funny to himself. Of course The Joker has been caught by the police and sent to justice, but he was always found not guilty by reason of insanity and sent to Arkham Asylum instead of getting the death penalty.

小丑瘋了，成了我們今天知道的邪惡的小丑。他也把責任推給蝙蝠俠。每個小丑所犯的罪，都是要得到蝙蝠俠的關注。從謀殺，盜竊，到恐怖主義，沒有一件是長尾外套、紫色西裝、條紋領帶、條紋褲、尖頭鞋的男人所害怕的。他曾經聲稱，他殺害了 2000 餘人。小丑是一個極端的心理變態，並認為他所做的一切是有趣和幽默的。然而，只有他一人覺得好笑。當然，小丑也曾經被警察抓，並送到矯正署，但他始終沒有被判重罪。他因為精神

錯亂而無罪，並被送往瘋人院，而不是死刑。

## ▶▶▶ 影子跟讀「短段落」練習 🎧 MP3 044

此部分為「**影子跟讀短段落練習❷**」，請重新播放音檔並完成試題，現在就一起動身，開始完成「**短段落練習❷**」吧！

No one really knows where this 1._____ skin, red lips, and 2._____ joker actually came from. There is one indication that says that the Joker quitted his 3._____ to become a stand-up 4._____ to support his 5._____. Economic conditions led to his 6._____ with a 7._____. Although the robbery was successful, the Joker fell into a giant 8._____ vat when he attempted to escape from Batman. The chemical inside the vat changed the whole look of Joker. Even worse, the Joker found out that both his wife and unborn child were dead due to an 9._____.

Every crime The Joker does is to get Batman's 10._____. From 11._____, theft to 12._____, nothing scares the man in the 13._____ suite with a long-tailed 14._____, the string tie, the striped pants, and the pointed-toe 15._____. He once claimed that he killed more than 16._____ people.

Joker is an extreme psychopath that thinks everything he does is funny and 17.＿＿＿＿＿＿＿＿. Of course The Joker has been caught by 18.＿＿＿＿＿＿＿＿ and sent to justice, but he was always found not guilty by reason of insanity and sent to Arkham 19.＿＿＿＿＿＿＿ instead of getting the 20.＿＿＿ ＿＿＿＿.

▶▶ 參考答案

| | |
|---|---|
| 1. bleached white | 2. green hair |
| 3. job | 4. comedian |
| 5. wife | 6. agreement |
| 7. robbery | 8. chemical |
| 9. accident | 10. attention |
| 11. murder | 12. terrorism |
| 13. purple | 14. jacket |
| 15. shoes | 16. 2000 |
| 17. humorous | 18. the police |
| 19. Asylum | 20. death penalty |

# 飛機＋原子＋常考名詞＝ Wonder Woman 神力女超人

▶▶ 影子跟讀「短段落」練習 🎧 MP3 045

此篇為「**影子跟讀短段落練習**」，規劃了由聽「**短段落**」的 shadowing 練習，強化考生定位和聆聽數個句子的專注力，聽 section 3 和 section 4 都覺得瞬間變得簡單，現在就一起動身，開始聽「**短段落**」！

A plane crash led to a forbidden relationship between Diana and Captain Steve Trevor. Nursing an unconscious man fostered the love. Diana didn't care and insisted to have a competition, a competition that will determine who is the strongest woman. Without a surprise, Diana won the competition and convinced her mother to return Steve Trevor back home. she was wearing the special dress made by her mother, and it was the Wonder Woman costume. The identity of Wonder Woman was born.

飛機失事使黛安娜和機長史蒂夫‧特雷弗發展了禁忌關係。照料昏迷不醒的男人助長了愛情。戴安娜也沒在意，堅持參加比賽，一個決定誰是最強女人的比賽。毫無意外，戴安娜贏得了比

賽，並說服她的母親，讓她帶史蒂夫· 特雷弗回家。她穿著由她的母親所做的特別服裝，這是神力女超人的服裝。神力女超人的身份就此誕生。

Wonder Woman has a couple of signature weapons. The Lasso of Truth compels all human beings who come into contact with it to tell the truth. A pair of indestructible bracelets can block and absorb the impact of incoming attacks and eventually deflect automatic weapon fire. She also has a magical sword that is sharp enough to cut the electrons off an atom. The tiara allows her to telepathically contact people, and it can also be used as a throwing weapon. She travels with her invisible and silent plane which is also controlled by her amazing tiara.

神力女超人有幾個標誌性的武器。真理的套索，可以迫使接觸到它的人說出一切真相。一對堅不可摧的手鐲，可以阻擋和吸收攻擊進來的影響，並最終轉移力量成為自動武器。她也有一把神奇且銳利的劍，使她可以削斷電子的原子。后冠使她與人心靈感應，也可以作為投擲武器。她的旅行，也是由她驚人的后冠控制她的無形且無聲的飛機。

此部分為「影子跟讀短段落練習❷」，請重新播放音檔並完成試題，現在就一起動身，開始完成「短段落練習❷」吧！

A 1.＿＿＿＿＿ led to a forbidden 2.＿＿＿＿＿ between Diana and Captain Steve Trevor. Nursing an unconscious man fostered the love. Diana didn't care and insisted to have a 3.＿＿＿＿＿, a competition that will determine who is the 4.＿＿＿＿＿. Without a surprise, Diana won the 5.＿＿＿＿＿ and convinced her mother to return Steve Trevor back home. she was wearing the 6.＿＿＿＿＿＿ made by her mother, and it was the Wonder Woman 7.＿＿＿＿＿＿. The 8.＿＿＿＿＿ of Wonder Woman was born.

Wonder Woman has a couple of signature 9.＿＿＿＿＿＿. The Lasso of Truth compels all human beings who come into contact with it to tell the 10.＿＿＿＿＿. A pair of indestructible 11.＿＿＿＿＿ can block and 12.＿＿＿＿＿＿ the impact of incoming attacks and eventually deflect automatic weapon 13.＿＿＿＿＿. She also has a magical sword that is sharp enough to cut the 14.＿＿＿＿＿ off an 15.＿＿＿＿＿. The tiara allows her to telepathically contact people, and it can also be used as a throwing weapon. She travels with her invisible and silent plane which is also controlled by her amazing 16.＿＿＿＿＿.

## ▶▶ 參考答案

| | |
|---|---|
| 1. plane crash | 2. relationship |
| 3. competition | 4. strongest woman |
| 5. competition | 6. special dress |
| 7. costume | 8. identity |
| 9. weapons | 10. truth |
| 11. bracelets | 12. absorb |
| 13. fire | 14. electrons |
| 15. atom | 16. tiara |

影子跟讀「短對話」

影子跟讀「短段落」

影子跟讀「長段落」

# 顏色＋男孩＋常考名詞－Superman超人 **❶**

▶ 影子跟讀「短段落」練習 🎧 MP3 046

此篇為「**影子跟讀短段落練習**」，規劃了由聽「**短段落**」的 shadowing 練習，強化考生定位和聆聽數個句子的專注力，聽 section 3 和 section 4 都覺得瞬間變得簡單，現在就一起動身，開始聽「**短段落**」！

"Faster than a speeding bullet. More powerful than a locomotive. Able to leap tall buildings in a single bound ... It's Superman!" This is the formulistic phrase when people describe Superman. Born on the alien planet Krypton, Kal-El, A.K.A Superman, is the son of Jor-El and Lara. When his parents became aware of Krypton's impending destruction, Jor-El started to build a spacecraft that would carry Kal-El to Earth. The spacecraft with Kal-El inside was launched right before Krypton exploded. His parents both died in the incident.

「比子彈更快，比火車更強大，能夠單一彈跳的躍上高層建築…他是超人！」這是當人們形容超人的制式化說法。出生於克利普頓星球的凱‧艾爾，又名超人，是喬‧艾爾和拉拉的兒子。

當他的父母知道克利普頓星球即將毀滅時，喬‧艾爾開始建造一個可以將凱‧艾爾帶到地球的太空船。就在克利普頓星球爆炸前，載著凱‧艾爾的太空船推進出發。他的父母均在事件中死亡。

The spacecraft landed in country side of the United States. Jonathan and Martha Kent found the spaceship and rescued Kal-El. They adopted the boy and renamed him Clark Kent.

太空船降落在美國的鄉村。喬納森和馬莎‧肯特發現了太空船並解救了凱‧艾爾。他們收養了這個男孩，並將他改名為克拉克‧肯特。

During his growth, his adoptive parents discovered that Clark has superpowers. The Kent's taught Clark to conceal his origins and use the power wisely and responsibly. After Clark became a grown man, he created the alter ego of Superman with the red and blue costume with a letter "S" on his chest and a cape.

在他的成長過程中，他的養父母發現了克拉克的超能力。肯特夫婦教導克拉克要隱瞞他的出身，並明智且有責任地使用他的超能力。克拉克成年後，他創造了超人的服裝，利用紅色和藍色搭配裝束，並在他的胸前和披風上放了一個字母「S」。

## ▶▶ 影子跟讀「短段落」練習 🎧 MP3 046

此部分為「影子跟讀短段落練習❷」，請重新播放音檔並完成試題，現在就一起動身，開始完成「短段落練習❷」吧！

"Faster than a speeding 1._____. More powerful than a 2._____. Able to leap 3._____ in a single bound ... It's Superman!" This is the formulistic 4._____ when people describe Superman. Born on the alien 5._____ Krypton, Kal-El, A.K.A Superman, is the son of Jor-El and Lara. When his parents became aware of Krypton's 6._____, Jor-El started to build a 7._____ that would carry Kal-El to Earth. His parents both died in the 8._____.They adopted the 9._____ and renamed him Clark Kent.

During his 10._____, his adoptive 11._____ discovered that Clark has superpowers. The Kent's taught Clark to 12._____ his origins and use the power wisely and responsibly. After Clark became a grown 13._____, he created the alter 14._____ of Superman with the 15._____ 16._____ with a letter "S" on his chest and a cape.

## ▶▶ 參考答案

| | |
|---|---|
| 1. bullet | 2. locomotive |
| 3. tall buildings | 4. phrase |
| 5. planet | 6. impending destruction |
| 7. spacecraft | 8. incident |
| 9. boy | 10. growth |
| 11. parents | 12. conceal |
| 13. man | 14. ego |
| 15. red and blue | 16. costume |

影子跟讀「短對話」

影子跟讀「短段落」

影子跟讀「長段落」

# 報紙＋顏色＋天文＋常考名詞－Superman超人 ❷

▶▶ 影子跟讀「短段落」練習 🎧 MP3 047

此篇為「影子跟讀短段落練習」，規劃了由聽「短段落」的 shadowing 練習，強化考生定位和聆聽數個句子的專注力，聽 section 3 和 section 4 都覺得瞬間變得簡單，現在就一起動身，開始聽「短段落」！

As Clark Kent, he works for a newspaper, wears eyeglasses, loose clothing and suits and has a soft voice. As Clark Kent, he always avoids violent confrontation. Instead, he slips away and changes into Superman and then starts the rescue or the battle. Clark works for the Daily Planet and is attracted to his colleague Lois Lane. Ironically, Lois is attracted to Superman. There were times that Lois suspected Clark is Superman, but Superman never admitted the fact. As a hero from a planet that does not exist anymore and does not have any survivors besides him, Superman oftentimes feels lonely deep down.

當是克拉克・肯特的身份時，他替報社工作，戴眼鏡，穿寬

鬆的衣服和西裝，具有柔和的聲音。克拉克・肯特總是避免暴力對抗。相反的，當他溜走變成超人後，他則開始搶救或戰鬥的行動。克拉克在每日星球報工作，並被他的同事露伊絲・蓮所吸引。諷刺的是，露伊絲喜歡的是超人。有幾次露伊絲懷疑克拉克就是超人，但超人卻從不承認這一件事。一個從已經不存在且沒有生還者的星球而來的英雄，超人內心常常感到孤單。

Superman's signature powers include flight, super-strength, invulnerability to non-magical attacks, super speed, heat-emitting, super healing, super-intelligence and super-breath. He also has x-ray, heat-emitting, telescopic and microscopic vision. He can even push planets around. He often time flies across the solar system to stop meteors from hitting the earth. He can also withstand nuclear blasts, fly into the sun, and survive in space without oxygen. Nothing can harm him, you might think. Actually, there is something! Superman is the most vulnerable to green Kryptonite radiation. When Superman is exposed to to green Kryptonite radiation, his powers will be nullified and he will feel pain and nausea.

超人著名的能力包括飛行、超有力、對於非魔法的攻擊刀槍不入、超高速、可以發熱、超強的癒合、超級智能和超級氣流。他也有 X 光、發熱、伸縮和微觀的視野。他甚至可以推行行星。他經常在整個太陽系飛行，以防流星隕石撞擊到地球。他也能承受核爆，飛入太陽，即使沒有氧氣也能在太空中生存。你可能會

認為沒有什麼能傷害他。其永存於人們心中的英雄霸主實有的！超人最容易受到綠色氪石輻射的傷害。當超人暴露在綠色氪石輻射中時，他的能力將無用，他會感到疼痛和噁心，最終還會死掉。

## ▶▶▶ 影子跟讀「短段落」練習　🎧 MP3 047

此部分為「**影子跟讀短段落練習❷**」，請重新播放音檔並完成試題，現在就一起動身，開始完成「**短段落練習❷**」吧！

As Clark Kent, he works for a 1._____, wears 2._____, loose clothing and suits and has a 3._____. As Clark Kent, he always avoids 4._____. Instead, he slips away and changes into Superman and then starts the rescue or the 5._____. Clark works for the Daily Planet and is attracted to his 6._____ Lois Lane. Ironically, Lois is attracted to Superman. There were times that Lois suspected Clark is Superman, but Superman never admitted the fact. As a hero from a 7._____ that does not exist anymore and does not have any 8._____ besides him, Superman oftentimes feels lonely deep down.

Superman's 9._____ powers include flight, super-strength, invulnerability to 10._____ attacks, super speed, heat-emitting, super healing, super-intelligence and super-breath. He also has x-ray, heat-emitting, telescopic and 11._____. He often time flies across the 12._____ to stop 13._____ from hitting the earth. He can also withstand 14._____, fly into the sun, and survive in space without 15._____. Actually, there is something! Superman is the most vulnerable to 16._____ Kryptonite 17._____. ......, his powers will be nullified and he will feel pain and 18._____.

## ▶▶ 參考答案

| | |
|---|---|
| 1. newspaper | 2. eyeglasses |
| 3. soft voice | 4. violent confrontation |
| 5. battle | 6. colleague |
| 7. planet | 8. survivors |
| 9. signature | 10. non-magical |
| 11. microscopic vision | 12. solar system |
| 13. meteors | 14. nuclear blasts |
| 15. oxygen | 16. green |
| 17. radiation | 18. nausea |

# 數字＋國名＋常考名詞－Iron Man 鋼鐵人 ❶

▶▶ 影子跟讀「短段落」練習　🎧 MP3 048

此篇為「**影子跟讀短段落練習**」，規劃了由聽「**短段落**」的 shadowing 練習，強化考生定位和聆聽數個句子的專注力，聽 section 3 和 section 4 都覺得瞬間變得簡單，現在就一起動身，開始聽「**短段落**」！

The son of Howard and Maria Stark, Anthony Edward Stark was born on Long Island. Stark's father was a successful and wealthy man and head of Stark Industries. Stark himself was a genius who entered MIT at the age of 15 and received masters of electrical engineering and physics. Unfortunately, both of his parents were killed in a car accident. Since then, Anthony inherited his father's company. While Anthony was visiting Vietnam, he got injured by a booby trap and was captured by enemy forces led by Wong-Chu.

霍華德和瑪麗亞・史塔克的兒子，安東尼・愛德華・史塔克出生在長島。史塔克的父親是一個成功且富有的男子和史塔克實業的老闆。史塔克是個天才，在 15 歲時進入麻省理工學院，並獲

得電氣工程和物理學的碩士。不幸的是，他的父母在一場車禍中喪生。此後，安東尼繼承了父親的公司。當安東尼訪問越南時，他因為詭雷而受傷，並被王秋所率領的敵軍所捕。

Wong-Chu forced Anthony to design and build weapons for him. Anthony refused. He was badly injured. Luckily, he met a Nobel Prize-winning physicist, Ho Yinsen, in the prison.

王秋逼迫安東尼替他設計和建造武器。安東尼拒絕。他受了重傷。幸運的是，他在監獄裡遇到了一位諾貝爾獎得主，物理學家何殷森。

Yinsen made a magnetic chest plate to keep the shrapnel from reaching Anthony's heart in order to keep him alive. They also secretly built a powered suit armor in order to escape from the prison. During the escape attempt, Yinsen sacrificed his life to save Anthony's escape. After Anthony got home, he discovered that there is no way he could remove the shrapnel from his chest. If he does, he will die. In order to live, he is forced to wear the armored chest plate beneath his clothe. The chest plate needs to be recharged every day. When Iron Man was discovered in public, Anthony told the public that Iron Man is just a robotic personal bodyguard.

影子跟讀「短對話」

影子跟讀「短段落」

影子跟讀「長段落」

殷森設計了一個具有磁性的裝甲，以防止砲彈碎片刺到安東尼的心臟。他們還偷偷內置動力裝甲，以利從監獄逃跑。在逃亡途中，殷森犧牲了自己的生命來拯救安東尼逃跑。安東尼回家後，他發現並沒有可以去除他的胸口砲彈碎片的方法。如果他這樣做，他將會死亡。為了生活，他被迫在衣服裡穿著裝甲護胸。裝甲每天需要充電。當鋼鐵人在公共場所被發現時，安東尼告訴大家鋼鐵人只是一個機器式的個人貼身保鏢。

## ▶▶▶ 影子跟讀「短段落」練習　🎧 MP3 048

　　此部分為「**影子跟讀短段落練習❷**」，請重新播放音檔並完成試題，現在就一起動身，開始完成「**短段落練習❷**」吧！

　　The 1._____ of Howard and Maria Stark, Anthony Edward Stark was born on 2._____. Stark's father was a successful and wealthy 3._____ and head of Stark Industries. Stark himself was a 4._____ who entered MIT at the age of 5._____ and received masters of 6._____ and 7._____. Unfortunately, both of his parents were killed in a 8._____. Since then, Anthony inherited his father's 9._____. While Anthony was visiting 10._____, he got injured by a booby trap and was captured by 11._____ led by Wong-Chu. Luckily, he met a Nobel Prize-winning 12._____, Ho Yinsen, in the prison.

Yinsen made a magnetic chest plate to keep the shrapnel from reaching Anthony's 13.＿＿＿＿＿＿＿ in order to keep him alive. They also secretly built a 14.＿＿＿＿＿＿＿ in order to escape from the 15.＿＿＿＿＿＿＿. After Anthony got home, he discovered that there is no way he could remove the shrapnel from his 16.＿＿＿＿＿＿＿. If he does, he will die. In order to live, he is forced to wear the armored chest plate beneath his 17.＿＿＿＿＿＿＿. When Iron Man was discovered in public, Anthony told the public that Iron Man is just a robotic 18.＿＿＿＿＿＿＿.

## ▶▶ 參考答案

| | |
|---|---|
| 1. son | 2. Long Island |
| 3. man | 4. genius |
| 5. 15 | 6. electrical engineering |
| 7. physics | 8. car accident |
| 9. company | 10. Vietnam |
| 11. enemy forces | 12. physicist |
| 13. heart | 14. powered suit armor |
| 15. prison | 16. chest |
| 17. clothe | 18. personal bodyguard |

# 秘書＋生物學＋常考名詞－Iron Man 鋼鐵人 ❷

▶▶ 影子跟讀「短段落」練習 🎧 MP3 049

　　此篇為「影子跟讀短段落練習」，規劃了由聽「短段落」的 shadowing 練習，強化考生定位和聆聽數個句子的專注力，聽 section 3 和 section 4 都覺得瞬間變得簡單，現在就一起動身，開始聽「短段落」！

　　No one had any doubt about what Anthony had said because he cultivates a public image of being a rich playboy. Only a couple of people know his secret identity – his personal chauffeur, Harold "Happy" Hogan, and secretary Virginia "Pepper" Potts.

　　沒有人對安東尼有任何的質疑，因為他的公眾形象是一名富有的花花公子。只有幾個人知道他的秘密身份－他的私人司機哈羅德「快樂」霍根和秘書弗吉尼亞「辣椒」波茨。

　　Like Batman, he uses his personal fortune to fight against illegal activities, striving to be environmentally responsible. His heart condition was cured by an artificial heart transplant. Without any supehuman power, he simply relies on his designed weapons. The most standard one has been the repulsor rays, fired through the palms of his gauntlets. He also has the uni-beam projector in his chest, pulse blots, an electromagnetic pulse generator and a defensive energy shield. The bleeding edge armor is stored in Anthony's bones and can be assembled and controlled by his thoughts.

如同蝙蝠俠，他使用自己的財富來打擊犯罪活動，也努力對環境負責。人工心臟治癒了他的心臟問題。不具有任何超能力，他僅仰賴他所設計的武器。最制式的是衝擊光束，是透過手套的手掌上釋放。他也有在他的胸口設計單束光炮、電磁衝波發射器以及能量護盾。內層儲存裝甲被存在安東尼的骨骼中，可組裝並透過他的思想來控制。

During a battle with the extremis - enhanced Mallen, Anthony was badly injured. To survive, he injected his nervous system with modified techno organic viruses which rewrote his biology. By doing so, he also gained an enhanced healing factor. He also is able to store some of the components of the armor-sheath in his body and can be recalled and extruded from his own skin.

在與絕境病毒強化後的敵手麥倫交戰後，安東尼受了重傷。為了生存，他在神經內注入改造過後的生化科技病毒，這改變了他的生物特徵。透過這樣做，他也得到了增強癒合的因子。他還

能夠將部分裝甲的組件存儲在他的身體裡，並可以被調用，從他自己的皮膚中擠出。

## ▶▶ 影子跟讀「短段落」練習　🎧 MP3 049

此部分為「影子跟讀短段落練習❷」，請重新播放音檔並完成試題，現在就一起動身，開始完成「短段落練習❷」吧！

No one had any doubt about what Anthony had said because he cultivates a 1.＿＿＿＿＿＿ of being a 2.＿＿＿＿＿＿＿. Only a couple of people know his 3.＿＿＿＿＿＿ – his 4.＿＿＿＿＿, Harold "Happy" Hogan, and 5.＿＿＿＿＿ Virginia "Pepper" Potts. Like Batman, he uses his 6.＿＿＿＿＿ to fight against 7.＿＿＿＿＿, striving to be 8.＿＿＿＿＿. His heart condition was cured by an 9.＿＿＿＿＿. Without any supehuman power, he simply relies on his 10.＿＿＿＿＿. The most standard one has been the repulsor rays, fired through the 11.＿＿＿＿＿ of his gauntlets. He also has the uni-beam projector in his 12.＿＿＿＿＿, pulse blots, an electromagnetic pulse generator and a defensive energy shield. The bleeding edge armor is stored in Anthony's 13.＿＿＿＿＿.

To survive, he injected his 14.＿＿＿＿＿ with modified techno 15.＿＿＿＿＿ which rewrote his 16.＿＿＿＿

_____. By doing so, he also gained an enhanced healing factor. He also is able to store some of the 17._____ of the armor-sheath in his body and can be recalled and extruded from his own 18._____.

## ▶▶ 參考答案

| | |
|---|---|
| 1. public image | 2. rich playboy |
| 3. secret identity | 4. personal chauffeur |
| 5. secretary | 6. personal fortune |
| 7. illegal activities | 8. environmentally responsible |
| 9. artificial heart transplant | 10. designed weapons |
| 11. palms | 12. chest |
| 13. bones | 14. nervous system |
| 15. organic viruses | 16. biology |
| 17. components | 18. skin |

# 國名＋語言＋常考名詞－Mandarin滿大人 ❶

▶▶ 影子跟讀「短段落」練習 🎧 MP3 050

此篇為「影子跟讀短段落練習」，規劃了由聽「短段落」的 shadowing 練習，強化考生定位和聆聽數個句子的專注力，聽 section 3 和 section 4 都覺得瞬間變得簡單，現在就一起動身，開始聽「短段落」！

Half Chinese and half English, Mandarin was born into a wealthy family in an unnamed village in mainland China before the Communist revolution. Even though Mandarin's father was considered one of the wealthiest people in China, he and his wife died soon after Mandarin was born. Mandarin was raised by his radical aunt who was embittered against the world. She spent every bit of the family fortune training Mandarin in science and combat. Mandarin became the master of what he has learned, but was penniless and unable to pay his taxes. Therefore, Mandarin was evicted from his own house by the government.

一半是中國人，一半英國人，滿大人出生在一個共產革命前

中國內的一個不知名村落的富裕家庭裡。儘管滿大人的父親被認為是最富有的中國人之一，他和他的妻子在滿大人出生後不久就去世了。滿大人是由他反世界的激進派阿姨所帶大。她花了家裡的每一分財產，在科學和格鬥上培訓滿大人。滿大人成為了這方面的菁英，但卻身無分文，無力支付稅金。因此，滿大人被政府驅逐出自己的房子。

　　Mandarin decided to explore the forbidden Valley of Spirits where no one has visited for centuries. He spent years there studying Makluan science and learning how to use ten rings he found within the starship of Axonn-Karr. Mandarin then returned back to civilization and started his journey to conquer the world. He swore he will crash the government, kill the ones who despise him, and eventually dominate the world. He knew that he needs the most advanced weapons to help him achieve his goals. Therefore, he was stealing American missiles and spy planes built by Anthony Stark. Of course Anthony could not let Mandarin ruin his reputation.

　　滿大人決定探索幾百年來從未有人走訪的禁谷。他花了幾年，學習麥卡倫科學，學習如何使用他在艾森卡爾的飛船內發現的十枚戒指。滿大人爾後返回文明，開始了他的旅程，征服世界。他發誓他要擊潰政府，殺死每一個曾經看不起他的那些人，並最終統一天下。他知道，他需要最先進的武器，以幫助他實現他的目標。因此，他偷了由安東尼・史塔克在美國製造的導彈和

間諜飛機。當然，安東尼不能讓滿大人毀了他的名聲。


## ▶▶ 影子跟讀「短段落」練習　🎧 MP3 050

　　此部分為「影子跟讀短段落練習❷」，請重新播放音檔並完成試題，現在就一起動身，開始完成「短段落練習❷」吧！


　　Half 1.＿＿＿＿＿＿ and half 2.＿＿＿＿＿＿, Mandarin was born into a 3.＿＿＿＿＿＿ family in an unnamed 4.＿＿＿＿＿＿ in mainland 5.＿＿＿＿＿＿ before the 6.＿＿＿＿＿＿. Mandarin was raised by his 7.＿＿＿＿＿＿ who was 8.＿＿＿＿＿＿ against the world. She spent every bit of the family fortune training Mandarin in 9.＿＿＿＿＿＿ and combat. Mandarin became the master of what he has learned, but was 10.＿＿＿＿＿＿ and unable to pay his 11.＿＿＿＿＿＿. Therefore, Mandarin was 12.＿＿＿＿＿＿ from his own 13.＿＿＿＿＿＿ by the government.

　　He spent years there studying Makluan science and learning how to use 14.＿＿＿＿＿＿ he found within the 15.＿＿＿＿＿＿ of Axonn-Karr. Mandarin then returned back to 16.＿＿＿＿＿＿ and started his 17.＿＿＿＿＿＿ to conquer the world. He knew that he needs the most 18.＿＿＿＿＿＿ to help him achieve his goals. Therefore, he was stealing 19.＿＿＿＿＿＿ and 20.＿＿＿＿＿＿ built by Anthony Stark. Of course Anthony could not let Mandarin ruin his reputation.

## ▶▶ 參考答案

| | |
|---|---|
| 1. Chinese | 2. English |
| 3. wealthy | 4. village |
| 5. China | 6. Communist revolution |
| 7. radical aunt | 8. embittered |
| 9. science | 10. penniless |
| 11. taxes | 12. evicted |
| 13. house | 14. ten rings |
| 15. starship | 16. civilization |
| 17. journey | 18. advanced weapons |
| 19. American missiles | 20. spy planes |

影子跟讀「短對話」

影子跟讀「短段落」

影子跟讀「長段落」

# 書籍＋溫度＋常考名詞－Aquaman水行俠 ❶

▶▶ 影子跟讀「短段落」練習 🎧 MP3 051

　　此篇為「**影子跟讀短段落練習**」，規劃了由聽「**短段落**」的 shadowing 練習，強化考生定位和聆聽數個句子的專注力，聽 section 3 和 section 4 都覺得瞬間變得簡單，現在就一起動身，開始聽「短段落」！

　　Born by the ocean, Arthur Curry is the son of Tom Curry, a lighthouse keeper, and Atlanna. Atlanna passed away when Arthur was a baby. His father, Tom, spent most of his time underwater as an undersea explorer. He found an ancient city in the depths where no one had ever penetrated. He believed it was the lost kingdom of Atlantis. Tom then spent most of his time in one of the palaces.

　　出生於海邊，亞瑟・柯瑞是看守燈塔者湯姆・柯瑞和亞特蘭那的兒子。亞特蘭那去世時，亞瑟還是個嬰兒。他的父親湯姆，花了他大部分時間在海底探險。他發現了一個古老的城市，在沒有人滲透的深處。他認為這是亞特蘭蒂斯的失落王國。湯姆當時花了他的大部分時間在其中一個宮殿之中。

In the palace, he found a lot of books and records which taught him ways to live under the ocean. Tom also trained Arthur ways to live and thrive under the water.

在宮中，他發現了大量的書籍和記錄，這些文獻教會他如何在海洋底下生活。湯姆也教育亞瑟在水底生活的方式，並在水中茁壯成長。

He has the ability to live in the depths of the ocean, breathe underwater, remain unaffected by the immense pressure and the cold temperatures of the ocean. He can also swim at the speed of 3,000 meters per second and can swim up Niagara Falls. He even withstands gun fire, sees in darkness and can hear limited sonar.

他可以住在海洋深處，在水裡呼吸，並且不會受到巨大的壓力和海洋低溫的影響。他還可以以每秒 3000 米的速度游泳，並逆游尼亞加拉大瀑布。他也可以防彈，在黑暗中看到事物，並可以聽到有限的聲納。

影子跟讀「短對話」

影子跟讀「短段落」

影子跟讀「長段落」

## ▶▶▶ 影子跟讀「短段落」練習　🎧 MP3 051

　　此部分為「影子跟讀短段落練習❷」，請重新播放音檔並完成試題，現在就一起動身，開始完成「短段落練習❷」吧！

　　Born by the ocean, Arthur Curry is the 1.＿＿＿＿＿＿ of Tom Curry, a 2.＿＿＿＿＿＿, and Atlanna. Atlanna passed away when Arthur was 3.＿＿＿＿＿＿. His father, Tom, spent most of his time 4.＿＿＿＿＿＿ as an 5.＿＿＿＿＿＿. He found an 6.＿＿＿＿＿＿ in the depths where no one had ever penetrated. He believed it was the lost 7.＿＿＿＿＿＿ of 8.＿＿＿＿＿＿. Tom then spent most of his time in one of the 9.＿＿＿＿＿＿.

　　In the palace, he found a lot of 10.＿＿＿＿＿＿ and 11.＿＿＿＿＿＿ which taught him ways to live under the ocean. He has the ability to live in the depths of the ocean, breathe underwater, remain 12.＿＿＿＿＿＿ by the 13.＿＿＿＿＿＿ and the 14.＿＿＿＿＿＿ of the ocean. He can also swim at the 15.＿＿＿＿＿＿ of 3,000 meters per second and can swim up 16.＿＿＿＿＿＿. He even withstands 17.＿＿＿＿＿＿, sees in darkness and can hear 18.＿＿＿＿＿＿.

## ▶▶ 參考答案

| | |
|---|---|
| 1. son | 2. lighthouse keeper |
| 3. a baby | 4. underwater |
| 5. undersea explorer | 6. ancient city |
| 7. kingdom | 8. Atlantis |
| 9. palaces | 10. books |
| 11. records | 12. unaffected |
| 13. immense pressure | 14. cold temperatures |
| 15. speed | 16. Niagara Falls |
| 17. gun fire | 18. limited sonar |

# 女人＋海洋＋常考名詞－Aquaman水行俠 **❷**

▶▶ 影子跟讀「短段落」練習　🎧 MP3 052

　　此篇為**「影子跟讀短段落練習」**，規劃了由聽**「短段落」**的 shadowing 練習，強化考生定位和聆聽數個句子的專注力，聽 section 3 和 section 4 都覺得瞬間變得簡單，現在就一起動身，開始聽**「短段落」**！

　　Besides all that, Arthur's most recognized power is the telepathic ability to communicate with anything related to the ocean, whether it's underneath or upon the sea. He is also capable of gathering all sea related lives together as a whole. Arthur eventually decided to use his power to keep the oceans in peace. He started to name himself Aquaman.

　　除了這一切，亞瑟最被認可的能力是與跟海洋有關的任何東西溝通，無論是否是在海上或海中的任何東西做心靈的感應。他還能集合海中生物作為一個整體。亞瑟最終決定用自己的力量來幫助維持海洋和平。他開始叫自己水行俠。

　　Although he can remain underwater for unlimited

time, Aquaman cannot remain on land for over one hour. Fortunately, Batman invented a water suit for Aquaman, so he is able to stay on land for an indefinite amount of time.

雖然他可以無時間限制的待在水中，但水行俠不能在陸地上待超過一小時。幸運的是，蝙蝠俠發明了一套水裝，讓水行俠能夠不受時間限制地留在陸地上。

Aquaman battled with several sea-based villains, including Nazi U-boat commanders, modern-day pirates, and many threats to aquatic life. Black Manta ordered to collect the blood of Arthur Curry to prove that he was actually an Atlantean. He failed in the mission and later on his father was killed by Aquaman. Black Manta held a grudge against Aquaman and started an endless revenge, while Orm Curry who is Aquaman's half-brother grew up as the trouble maker and lived in the shadow of his brother. Since Tom Curry's mother is an ordinary woman, he does not possess any superhuman strength. His jealousy towards Aquaman led him to become Aquaman's nemesis, Ocean Master.

與水行俠交手的幾個海基惡棍，其中包括了納粹潛艇指揮官、現代海盜以及水生生物的許多威脅。黑色曼塔奉命收集亞瑟‧柯瑞的血來證明他確實是亞特蘭蒂斯的一員。他的任務失敗，他的父親也被水行俠所殺害。黑色曼塔痛恨水行俠，並開始

了無休止的報復。而奧姆‧柯瑞是水行俠同父異母的弟弟，一個成長在哥哥影子裡的麻煩製造者。因為湯姆‧柯瑞的母親是普通人類，他不具有任何超能力特質。他對水行俠的忌妒導致他成了水行俠的剋星，海洋大師。

## ▶▶ 影子跟讀「短段落」練習 🎧 MP3 052

此部分為「影子跟讀短段落練習❷」，請重新播放音檔並完成試題，現在就一起動身，開始完成「短段落練習❷」吧！

Besides all that, Arthur's most recognized power is the 1.＿＿＿＿＿＿ ability to 2.＿＿＿＿＿＿ with anything related to the 3.＿＿＿＿＿＿, whether it's underneath or upon the sea. Arthur eventually decided to use his power to keep the oceans in 4.＿＿＿＿＿＿. Although he can remain 5.＿＿＿＿＿＿ for unlimited time, Aquaman cannot remain on 6.＿＿＿＿＿＿ for over one hour. Fortunately, Batman invented 7.＿＿＿＿＿＿ for Aquaman, so he is able to stay on land for an 8.＿＿＿＿＿＿ amount of time.

Aquaman battled with several sea-based 9.＿＿＿＿＿＿, including Nazi U-boat 10.＿＿＿＿＿＿, modern-day 11.＿＿＿＿＿＿, and many threats to 12.＿＿＿＿＿＿ life. Black Manta ordered to 13.＿＿＿＿＿＿ the blood of Arthur Curry to prove that he was actually an Atlantean. He failed in the 14.＿＿＿＿＿＿ and later on his father was killed by Aquaman. Black Manta held a 15._____ against Aquaman and started an endless 16._____. Since Tom Curry's mother is an 17._____, he does not possess any 18._____. His 19._____ towards Aquaman led him to become Aquaman's 20._____, Ocean Master.

▶▶ 參考答案

| | |
|---|---|
| 1. telepathic | 2. communicate |
| 3. ocean | 4. peace |
| 5. underwater | 6. land |
| 7. a water suit | 8. indefinite |
| 9. villains | 10. commanders |
| 11. pirates | 12. aquatic |
| 13. collect | 14. mission |
| 15. grudge | 16. revenge |
| 17. ordinary woman | 18. superhuman strength |
| 19. jealousy | 20. nemesis |

影子跟讀「短對話」

影子跟讀「短段落」

影子跟讀「長段落」

# 地名＋血液＋常考名詞－Black Manta黑色曼塔 ❶

▶ 影子跟讀「短段落」練習 🎧 MP3 053

　　此篇為「**影子跟讀短段落練習**」，規劃了由聽「**短段落**」的 shadowing 練習，強化考生定位和聆聽數個句子的專注力，聽 section 3 和 section 4 都覺得瞬間變得簡單，現在就一起動身，開始聽「**短段落**」！

　　On an ordinary day, while a sea-loving boy in Baltimore was enjoying his day by the ocean, he was kidnapped by some guys. He was enslaved on a ship, feeling so hopeless until he saw Aquaman and his dolphin friends. The little boy sent many signals to Aquaman expecting his rescue, but his hope was shattered because Aquaman didn't see him. He started to hate the ocean and Aquaman, resolving to become the master of the sea. After he grew up, he became a ruthless treasure hunter and mercenary.

　　在巴爾的摩的一個平凡日子，一位熱愛海洋的小男孩正在海邊享受他的光，他被幾個人綁架了。他在船上被迫做奴役的工作，感到希望渺茫，直到他看見水行俠和他的海豚朋友。小男孩

傳遞許多訊號給水行俠，期待他的救援，但卻希望破滅，因為水行俠沒看見他。他開始討厭海洋和水行俠，下定決心要成為大海的主人。他長大後，成為了一個無情的尋寶獵人和傭兵。

He designed his own wetsuit with a bug-eyed helmet which can shoot blasting rays from its eyes. He also started to call himself Black Manta. During most of his time, he scavenges and explores the depths of the ocean trying to find the long lost relics and powerful mythical items. One time, he was hired by Stephen Shin to collect a sample of Arthur Curry's blood. Black Manta initiated an attack while Arthur and his father were out to the sea. Although his father, Tom Curry, fought back, he suffered from a heart attack and ultimately died.

　　他設計了自己的潛水衣與有著如蟲眼讓他可以發射爆破射線的鋼盔。他也開始稱自己為黑色曼塔。在他的大部分時間裡，他在海洋裡拾荒，試圖尋找失蹤多年的文物和強大的神話寶物。有一次，他被史蒂芬・辛聘請收集亞瑟・柯瑞的血液樣本。黑色曼塔在亞瑟和他的父親出海時發起攻擊他們。雖然他的父親湯姆・柯瑞，展開反擊，但因心臟病發最終死亡。

影子跟讀「短對話」

影子跟讀「短段落」

影子跟讀「長段落」

# 影子跟讀「短段落」練習 🎧 MP3 053

此部分為「**影子跟讀短段落練習❷**」，請重新播放音檔並完成試題，現在就一起動身，開始完成「**短段落練習❷**」吧！

On an 1.＿＿＿＿＿ day, while a 2.＿＿＿＿＿ boy in 3.＿＿＿＿＿ was enjoying his day by the 4.＿＿＿＿＿＿, he was 5.＿＿＿＿＿ by some guys. He was enslaved on a 6.＿＿＿＿＿, feeling so 7.＿＿＿＿＿ until he saw Aquaman and his 8.＿＿＿＿＿ friends. The little boy sent many 9.＿＿＿＿＿ to Aquaman expecting his 10.＿＿＿＿＿＿, but his hope was 11.＿＿＿＿＿ because Aquaman didn't see him. After he grew up, he became a ruthless 12.＿＿＿＿＿ and mercenary.

He designed his own wetsuit with a bug-eyed 13.＿＿＿＿＿ which can shoot blasting rays from its 14.＿＿＿＿＿. He also started to call himself Black Manta. During most of his time, he scavenges and explores the depths of the ocean trying to find the 15.＿＿＿＿＿ and powerful 16.＿＿＿＿＿ items. One time, he was hired by Stephen Shin to collect a 17.＿＿＿＿＿ of Arthur Curry's 18.＿＿＿＿＿. Although his 19.＿＿＿＿＿, Tom Curry, fought back, he suffered from a 20.＿＿＿＿＿ and ultimately died.

228

## ▶▶ 參考答案

| | |
|---|---|
| 1. ordinary | 2. sea-loving |
| 3. Baltimore | 4. ocean |
| 5. kidnapped | 6. ship |
| 7. hopeless | 8. dolphin |
| 9. signals | 10. rescue |
| 11. shattered | 12. treasure hunter |
| 13. helmet | 14. eyes |
| 15. long-lost relics | 16. mythical |
| 17. sample | 18. blood |
| 19. father | 20. heart attack |

影子跟讀「短對話」

影子跟讀「短段落」

影子跟讀「長段落」

# 靈魂＋套裝＋走私＋常考名詞－Black Manta黑色曼塔 ❷

▶▶ 影子跟讀「短段落」練習　🎧 MP3 054

　　此篇為「**影子跟讀短段落練習**」，規劃了由聽「**短段落**」的 shadowing 練習，強化考生定位和聆聽數個句子的專注力，聽 section 3 和 section 4 都覺得瞬間變得簡單，現在就一起動身，開始聽「**短段落**」！

　　Aquaman's revenge later on accidentally killed Black Manta's father, resulting in the circle of vengeance. Manta first kidnapped Aquaman's wife, Mera, and their baby, Aquababy. He defeated Aquaman and turned him over to King Karshon. He then killed Aquababy in front of Aquaman. Aquaman was sad and angry. He hunted Manta down and nearly killed him. Instead, he decided to turn him over to the authorities. When Manta was released, he didn't regret anything he had done.

　　水行俠稍後復仇，在意外之下水行俠失手殺死了黑色曼塔的父親，復仇的輪迴從此開始。曼塔首先綁架了水行俠的妻子梅拉，和他的寶貝水寶寶。他擊敗了水行俠並且把他交給凱森國王。然後，他在水行俠面前殺死了水寶寶。水行俠既難過又生

氣。他捉到曼塔，且幾乎殺了他。然而，他決定把他交給當局。
曼塔被釋放時，他對自己所做的事情並不後悔。

　　Although, he gave up his thought on taking Aquaman down. Instead, Manta agreed to sell his soul to Neron for power and started to do drug smuggling and some shady works in Star City. Manda even approached Aquaman to work with him. Of course Aquaman wouldn't agree. Black Manta then attacked Sub Diego and nearly killed Captain Marley. Aquaman set several predatory forms of sea-life on him to kill him. Black Manta used an electrical charge in his suit to fend off his attackers and somehow managed to survive.

　　雖然，他放棄了打敗水行俠的想法。反之，曼塔同意將他靈魂出售給內隆以得到能力，並開始做毒品走私，並在星城裡做一些見不得人的事。曼達甚至找上水行俠與他合作。當然，水行俠不會同意。黑色曼塔隨後攻擊了狄亞哥，並險些殺死馬利隊長。水行俠爾後在海上設置了幾種形式，企圖殺了他。黑色曼達在他的衣服裡設計了電荷用來抵擋他的攻擊者，總算生存下來。

影子跟讀「短對話」

影子跟讀「短段落」

影子跟讀「長段落」

此部分為「影子跟讀短段落練習❷」，請重新播放音檔並完成試題，現在就一起動身，開始完成「**短段落練習❷**」吧！

　　Aquaman's 1.＿＿＿＿＿＿＿ later on 2.＿＿＿＿＿＿＿ killed Black Manta's father, resulting in the circle of 3.＿＿＿ ＿＿＿＿＿. Manta first 4.＿＿＿＿＿＿＿ Aquaman's wife, Mera, and their baby, Aquababy. He defeated Aquaman and turned him over to King Karshon. He then killed Aquababy in front of Aquaman. He hunted Manta down and nearly killed him. Instead, he decided to turn him over to 5.＿＿＿＿＿＿ ＿. When Manta was 6.＿＿＿＿＿＿＿, he didn't regret any-thing he had done.

　　Although, he gave up his 7.＿＿＿＿＿＿＿ on taking Aquaman down. Instead, Manta agreed to sell his 8.＿＿＿＿ ＿＿＿＿ to Neron for 9.＿＿＿＿＿＿＿ and started to do 10.＿ ＿＿＿＿＿＿＿＿ and some shady works in Star City. Manda even 11.＿＿＿＿＿＿ Aquaman to work with him. Black Manda then 12.＿＿＿＿＿＿＿ Sub Diego and nearly killed Captain Marley. Aquaman set several 13.＿＿＿＿＿＿＿ forms of sea-life on him to kill him. Black Manda used an 14.＿＿＿＿＿＿ ＿ in his 15.＿＿＿＿＿＿＿ to fend off his 16.＿＿＿＿＿＿＿ and somehow managed to survive.

## ▶▶ 參考答案

| | |
|---|---|
| 1. revenge | 2. accidentally |
| 3. vengeance | 4. kidnapped |
| 5. the authorities | 6. released |
| 7. thought | 8. soul |
| 9. power | 10. drug smuggling |
| 11. approached | 12. attacked |
| 13. predatory | 14. electrical charge |
| 15. suit | 16. attackers |

# 洞穴＋國名＋醫生＋常考名詞－Thor雷神索爾

▶ 影子跟讀「短段落」練習　🎧 MP3 055

　　此篇為「影子跟讀短段落練習」，規劃了由聽「短段落」的 shadowing 練習，強化考生定位和聆聽數個句子的專注力，聽 section 3 和 section 4 都覺得瞬間變得簡單，現在就一起動身，開始聽「短段落」！

　　During Thor's upbringing, Odin decided to send his son to earth to learn humility. He placed Thor into the body of Donald Blake, a partially disabled medical student. At that time, Thor lost his memories of godhood, and became a doctor in Norway. When Thor witnessed the arrival of an alien, he ran away, carelessly falling into a cave, where he discovered his hammer Mjolnir. He stroked it against a rock, and he transformed into the Thunder God.

　　在索爾的成長過程中，奧丁決定送兒子到地球去學習謙虛。他讓雷神成為一個部份殘疾的醫學系學生，唐納德·布萊克。當時，雷神失去了當神的記憶，而成為挪威的醫生。當索爾親眼目睹了一個外星人的到來。他逃跑，而不慎掉進一個山洞裡。在那

裡，他發現他的錘子雷神之鎚。他將它敲向石頭，他便轉變成雷神。

Thor started his double life, spending most of his time treating the ill in a private practice, and at the same time fighting evils to help humanity. During his practice, he fell in love with the nurse, Jane Foster, who is a normal human being. Thor wanted to marry Jane, but Odin rejected the request. Thor disobeyed his father and refused to return to Asgard. Odin eventually gave in and allowed Thor to date Jane Foster under the condition that she passes a trial. Foster's failing in the test made Thor understand that she is very much different from him.

索爾開始了他的雙重生活。他將大部分時間花費在私人診所治療病人。與此同時，他打擊犯罪幫助人類。在他的工作中，他愛上了一位普通人的護士，珍·福斯特。索爾想娶珍，但奧丁拒絕了這一個要求。索爾違背了他的父親，並拒絕返回仙宮。奧丁最終放棄，只要珍通過考驗，就允許索爾與珍在一起。福斯特未能通過試驗使索爾了解到珍·福斯特與他是有很大區別的。

影子跟讀「短對話」

影子跟讀「短段落」

影子跟讀「長段落」

此部分為「影子跟讀短段落練習❷」，請重新播放音檔並完成試題，現在就一起動身，開始完成「**短段落練習❷**」吧！

During Thor's 1.＿＿＿＿＿＿, Odin decided to send his son to 2.＿＿＿＿＿ to learn 3.＿＿＿＿＿. He placed Thor into the body of Donald Blake, a partially disabled 4.＿＿＿＿＿＿. At that time, Thor lost his 5.＿＿＿＿＿ of godhood, and became a 6.＿＿＿＿＿ in 7.＿＿＿＿＿. When Thor witnessed the arrival of an 8.＿＿＿＿＿, he ran away, carelessly falling into a 9.＿＿＿＿＿, where he discovered his 10.＿＿＿＿＿ Mjolnir. He stroked it against 11.＿＿＿＿＿.

Thor started his 12.＿＿＿＿＿ life, spending most of his time treating the ill in a 13.＿＿＿＿＿, and at the same time fighting evils to help humanity. During his practice, he fell in love with 14.＿＿＿＿＿, Jane Foster, who is a normal human being. Thor wanted to marry Jane, but Odin rejected the 15.＿＿＿＿＿. Thor disobeyed his father and refused to return to Asgard. Odin eventually gave in and allowed Thor to date Jane Foster under the condition that she passes 16.＿＿＿＿＿. Foster's failing in the 17.＿＿＿＿＿ made Thor 18.＿＿＿＿＿ that she is very much different from him.

## ▶▶ 參考答案

| | |
|---|---|
| 1. upbringing | 2. earth |
| 3. humility | 4. medical student |
| 5. memories | 6. doctor |
| 7. Norway | 8. alien |
| 9. cave | 10. hammer |
| 11. a rock | 12. double |
| 13. private practice | 14. the nurse |
| 15. request | 16. a trial |
| 17. test | 18. understand |

# 數字＋月份＋國名＋生物學專業字 ❶－無尾熊

▶▶ 影子跟讀「實戰練習」　🎧 MP3 056

　　此篇為**「影子跟讀實戰練習」**，規劃了由聽**「實際考試長度的英文內容」**的 shadowing 練習，經由先前的兩個部份的練習，已能逐步掌握聽一定句數的英文內容，現在經由實際考試長度的聽力內容來練習，讓耳朵適應聽這樣長度的英文內容，提升在考場時的答題**穩定度**和**適應性**，進而獲取理想成績，現在就一起動身，開始由聽**「實戰練習」**！（如果聽這部份且跟讀練習的難度還是太高請重複前兩個部份的練習數次後再來做這部分的練習喔！）

　　Koalas are recognised as symbol of Australia, but the species face many threats in this modernised world. Land exploitation in areas where koalas used to live has posed various risks to this cute creature. Urbanization is depriving and fragmenting koala habitat; human-induced threats such as vehicle strikes or domestic dog attacks are also threatening koala's life. It is also believed the increasing prevalence of koala's diseases are to some extent due to the stress caused by human activities.

　　無尾熊是澳洲公認的象徵，但是此物種在現代化世界中面臨許多威脅。無尾熊過去棲息的地方遭受的土地過度利用對這個可

愛的生物造成不同的風險威脅。都市化正剝奪和肢解著無尾熊的棲息地。人類引起的威脅像是汽車攻擊或家庭飼養的狗攻擊正威脅著無尾熊的生命。據說，無尾熊疾病的逐漸盛行某些程度上是由於人類活動所引起的壓力。

Some koalas live in the sanctuary where they are cared by the experienced staff. While most koalas live in the wild, they are easily recognized by their appearance and the habitat they are from. Koalas may be given a nickname by local residents if they show up frequently in the neighborhood, so they are more like human's pets rather than wild animals. People enjoy seeing koalas and they make lots of effort to protect them, such as planting trees and controlling their dogs.

有些無尾熊生活在保護區，在那裡受到具經驗的員工照顧著。雖然大多數的無尾熊生活在野外，能由外表輕易地辨識出牠們和牠們所處的棲息所在地。如果牠們頻繁地出現在社區的話，當地居民可能給予無尾熊暱稱。所以，牠們更像是人類的寵物而非野生動物。人們喜愛看到無尾熊，而他們為了保護無尾熊做了許多努力，例如植樹和控制他們的狗狗。

The biggest threat to koala's existence is habitat destruction, and following this, the most serious threat is death from car hits. I'm going to talk about the koala and the car accident. A koala hit by vehicle could be killed straight away or suffering serious injuries. The figure from the Australian Wildlife Hospital and another koala rescue center shows that 3792 koalas were taken to the hospitals between 1997 and 2008, and 85% of the injured koalas died after emergency procedures. This number is only the ones that have been calculated, so at least more than 300 koalas are killed each year by motor vehicles.

無尾熊生存中最大的威脅是棲地破壞，接續這個的原因，最嚴重的威脅是汽車撞擊所造成的死亡。我即將會談論到無尾熊和汽車意外。無尾熊被汽車撞到時可能即刻死亡或者遭受到嚴重的傷害。澳洲野生生物醫院和另一個無尾熊拯救中心的數據顯示出在 1997 年到 2008 年間有 3792 隻無尾熊帶往醫院且 85%的受傷無尾熊在緊急程序後死亡。這個僅是已經計算過後的數字，所以在每年至少有超過 300 隻無尾熊因汽車意外而死亡。

On June 11 2015, a 6-month-old baby koala clung to his mother during her life-saving surgery after she was hit by a car in Brisbane, Australia. The photo of the baby koala with Lizzy has attracted thousands of views. The mother Lizzy suffered severe injuries including facial trauma and a collapsed lung. The baby koala stayed by his mom's side throughout the entire operation. Luckily Lizzy started recovering after the surgery. How to prevent this kind of situation from happening in the first place has raised the public awareness.

在 2015 年 6 月 11 日，在牠母親於澳洲的布里斯本受到汽

車撞擊後，六個月大的無尾熊，於母親的急救手術期間緊抓著牠母親。無尾熊嬰兒的照片與麗茲已吸引了數千的觀看數。母親麗茲遭受到嚴重的傷害，包含臉部創傷和肺部衰竭。無尾熊嬰兒在整個手術期間都待在自己母親身旁。幸運的是，麗茲在手術後開始康復。首先關於如何使這樣的情況免於發生已經引起大眾的意識。

The Australia government has made a good effort to protect koala form car accidents. When you drive in Queensland, sometimes you can see an overpass built on top of a road. The over-bridge is the koala-crossing infra-structure. The state government has made guidelines for koala safety and required in areas where traffic flow pose risks to koalas, facilities assisting safe koala movement should be built.

澳洲政府已經做了充分的努力來保護無尾熊免於汽車意外。當你行駛在昆士蘭州，有時候你可以目睹在道路上方的高架橋。高架橋是無尾熊跨越的交通建設。州政府對於無尾熊的安全已經制定了指導方針而且要求交通流動會對於無尾熊造成威脅的地區，應該要建造協助無尾熊能安全移動的設施。

At individual level, although it may seem that there is not much we can do since the wild animals cannot be restricted from rushing out onto a road. There are still several things drivers can do to protect koalas, including obeying the speed limit, watching for koala crossing signs,

影子跟讀「短對話」

影子跟讀「短段落」

影子跟讀「長段落」

slowing down if they see koalas crossing, especially during the night, and report injured or dead koala if they see one. Wildlife-friendly driving would benefit koalas. The risk of hitting a koala can be reduced by avoid driving in areas where koalas appear. Driving slowly within the speed limit and scanning the roadside for anything that may move onto the road have a significant preventive effect.

在個人階段，儘管可能看起來沒有什麼是我們所能做的，因為無法限制野生動物不往路上衝去。仍有幾件事是駕駛能做以保護無尾熊的，包括遵守速限、觀看無尾熊跨越標誌、如果他們看到無尾熊跨越道路時減速，特別是在夜晚的時候，且如果他們看到時，舉報受傷或死亡的無尾熊。對野生生物友善的駕駛對無尾熊有益。在無尾熊出現的地方，牠們被撞到的風險會因此而降低。在速限內緩慢駕駛和掃描道路旁的任何可能出現在道路中的物件對於預防有顯著的成效。

Koalas can sleep up to twenty hours per day and not come to the ground very often. However, nowadays their habitat is fragmented by development. So they have to cross roads to reach some of the food trees. Koala crossing signs is a good indicator to inform drivers that have entered koala's territory. The peak time for them to move across road is most likely to be between July and September usually during the night. If driving through koala habitat during 'koala peak hour', drivers should slow down and check the roadside for koalas and other wild animals.

　　無尾熊每天能睡長達 24 小時且不常來到地面上。然而，現今牠們的棲息地受到土地開發而支離破碎了。所以牠們必須要越過道路抵達一些有食物的樹上。無尾熊跨越的標誌是告知駕駛已抵達無尾熊領域的一項好的指標。對他們來說越過道路的尖峰時刻最有可能是在七月和九月間，通常發生在夜晚。如果在無尾熊頂峰時刻行駛在無尾熊棲地，駕駛應該要減速且查看道路旁是否有無尾熊和其他野生動物。

During the night, koalas crossing the road would have eye shining. Their eyes reflect the headlights of coming vehicles, which would alert drivers. Driving slowly will give drivers enough time to reflect and avoid the hit. Animals' action would be unpredictable since they might become temporarily blind when confronted by bright light at night, but slowing down can give them time to get off the road.

　　在夜晚，無尾熊越過道路時會有眼睛閃耀的情況。牠們的眼睛對通行的車輛的車頭燈會反射出光亮，此能提醒駕駛。緩慢行駛會給予駕駛足夠的時間去反應和避免撞擊。動物的行動是難以預測的，因為當在夜晚時遭遇到亮光時，牠們可能轉變成短暫性地失明，但減速能給予牠們更多的時間離開道路。

What could people do if they see a koala accidentally or encounter an injured koala? It is recommended carry-

影子跟讀「短對話」

影子跟讀「短段落」

影子跟讀「長段落」

ing an old towel or blanket in the car. So the injured koala could be wrapped and moved out off the road. In addition, local wildlife care groups or vet surgerons can be contacted. Most importantly, people should always consider their own safety before intervening, cars need to be parked safely with hazard lights on to alert other drivers. Call the wildlife care groups if you are sure what actions to take. People who are interested in caring for the sick koalas can even attend certain training programs on wildlife rehabilitation to get useful information.

如果人們意外地看到無尾熊或遇到受傷的無尾熊，該怎麼辦呢？建議在車子裡攜帶舊毛巾或毯子。如此一來，受傷的無尾熊就能包裹在裏頭或被移開道路上。此外，能連繫當地的野生生物照護團體或外科獸醫。更重要的是，人們應該在干預前，總先考量到自身安全，汽車需要安全地停靠以危急燈警示其他駕駛。致電野生生物照護團體，如果你確定該採取的行動。人們對於照護生病的無尾熊有興趣的話甚至能夠參加特定的野生動物復健的訓練節目以獲取有用的資訊。

### ▶▶ 影子跟讀「實戰練習」　🎧 MP3 056

此部分為「影子跟讀實戰練習 ❷」，請重新播放音檔並完成試題，除了能提升並修正拼寫能力外，也可以藉由音檔注意自己專注力和定位聽力訊息部份，走神或定位錯都會影響在實際考場中的表現，

尤其在 section 3 和 4 影響的得分會更明顯，現在就一起動身，開始完成「**實戰練習 ❷**」吧！

1._____ in areas where koalas used to live has posed various risks to this cute creature. 2._____ is depriving and fragmenting koala habitat; human-induced threats such as vehicle strikes or domestic dog attacks are also threatening koala's life. Some koalas live in the 3._____ where they are cared by the experienced staff. Koalas may be given a 4._____ by local residents if they show up frequently in the neighborhood.

The biggest threat to koala's existence is 5._____, and following this, the most serious threat is death from car hits. I'm going to talk about the koala and the car accident. The figure from the Australian Wildlife Hospital and another koala rescue center shows that 6._____ koalas were taken to the hospitals between 1997 and 2008, and 85% of the injured koalas died after emergency procedures. On June 11 2015, a 6-month-old baby koala clung to his mother during her 7._____ after she was hit by a car in Brisbane, Australia. The mother Lizzy suffered severe injuries including 8._____ and a collapsed lung.

The Australia government has made a good effort to protect koala form car accidents. When you drive in 9._____, sometimes you can see an 10._____ built

on top of a road. The over-bridge is the 11._____.
There are still several things drivers can do to protect koalas, including obeying the 12._____, watching for
koala crossing signs, slowing down if they see koalas crossing, especially during the night, and report injured or dead
koala if they see one. 13._____ would benefit koalas. Driving slowly within the speed limit and scanning the
roadside for anything that may move onto the road have a
significant 14._____.

Koalas can sleep up to 15._____ per day and not
come to the ground very often. 16._____ is a good
indicator to inform drivers that have entered koala's 17.___
_____. The peak time for them to move across road is
most likely to be between 18._____ usually during
the night. If driving through koala habitat during 'koala peak
hour', drivers should slow down and check the roadside for
koalas and other wild animals.

During the night, koalas crossing the road would have
19._____. Their eyes reflect the 20._____ of
coming vehicles, which would alert drivers.

It is recommended carrying an old 21._____ in
the car. So the injured koala could be wrapped and moved
out off the road. In addition, local wildlife care groups or
22._____ can be contacted. Most importantly, peo-

ple should always consider their own safety before intervening, cars need to be parked safely with 23.＿＿＿＿＿＿＿ on
to alert other drivers. People who are interested in caring
for the sick koalas can even attend certain training programs
on 24.＿＿＿＿＿＿＿ to get useful information.

## ▶▶ 參考答案

| | |
|---|---|
| 1. Land exploitation | 2. Urbanization |
| 3. sanctuary | 4. nickname |
| 5. habitat destruction | 6. 3792 |
| 7. life-saving surgery | 8. facial trauma |
| 9. Queensland | 10. overpass |
| 11. koala-crossing infrastructure | 12. speed limit |
| 13. Wildlife-friendly driving | 14. preventive effect |
| 15. twenty hours | 16. Koala crossing signs |
| 17. territory | 18. July and September |
| 19. eye shining | 20. headlights |
| 21. towel or blanket | 22. vet surgeons |
| 23. hazard lights | 24. wildlife rehabilitation |

影子跟讀「短對話」

影子跟讀「短段落」

影子跟讀「長段落」

# 數字＋生態學和海洋生物學專業字 ❶ － 鯨魚

▶▶ 影子跟讀「實戰練習」　🎧 MP3 057

此篇為「**影子跟讀實戰練習**」，規劃了由聽「**實際考試長度的英文內容**」的 shadowing 練習，經由先前的兩個部份的練習，已能逐步掌握聽一定句數的英文內容，現在經由實際考試長度的聽力內容來練習，讓耳朵適應聽這樣長度的英文內容，提升在考場時的答題**穩定度**和**適應性**，進而獲取理想成績，現在就一起動身，開始由聽「**實戰練習**」！（如果聽這部份且跟讀練習的難度還是太高請重複前兩個部份的練習數次後再來做這部分的練習喔！）

Hi everyone, the topic our group selected for the wild-life case study is the whale. Now I will first present the general features and several species of whales then my group mates will continue with more detailed information.

嗨，各位好，我們這組所選的野生生物研究主題是鯨魚。現在我將首先呈現大致上的特徵和幾種鯨魚種類，然後我的組員夥伴會以更多細節資訊接續報告。

There are more than 90 species of whales, all whale species can be categorised into baleen whales and toothed whales. The baleen whales eat by swimming slowly through fish-rich water and straining food into their mouth. And toothed whales as their names indicate, have teeth. Whales live in marine environment and they are mammals. Just like the continental mammals, whales are also viviparous, which means they reproduce by giving birth to a calf rather than eggs, which leads to fewer off-spring and longer-lived individuals. Whales breathe with their lungs, and they all have blowholes positioned on top of their head. They breathe in air through the blowholes when they are on the water surface and close it up when they dive. All mammals need to sleep, but whales have to be awake all the time to maintain breath. So whales have a special sleep pattern: half of their brain falls asleep while the other half keeps awake, that makes whales to sleep 24 hours per day.

　　世界上有超過 90 種的鯨魚，所有鯨魚物種都能分類成有鬚鯨和齒鯨。鬚鯨藉由緩慢游進魚類豐富的水域，然後將食物拖進牠們口中的方式進食。而齒鯨則是如他們名字所示，有著牙齒。鯨魚居住在海洋環境而且牠們是哺乳類動物。如同地面上的補乳類動物，鯨魚同樣是胎生動物，這意謂著他們以產下幼子的方式繁殖，而非生蛋的形式，這也導致生產出較少的後代和較長壽的個體。鯨魚以肺部呼吸，而他們在頭部頂端裝置著噴水孔。當牠們在水面上或靠近水面而潛入時，鯨魚透過噴水孔吸入空氣。所有的哺乳類動物需要睡覺，但是鯨魚必須總是醒著以維持呼吸。所以鯨魚有著特別的睡眠形式：有一半部的腦部睡著，而另一半部

的腦部持續醒著，這使得鯨魚每天能睡眠 24 小時。

Whales have very advanced hearing and they can hear from miles away. They produce low frequency sound, which can be detected over large distances. Now many species of whales are declared as endangered. Apart from human activities, such as illegal whaling, these animals could collide with ships or become entangled with fishing nets. They are also threatened by pollution and habitat loss from climate change. Now I will briefly talk about four types of baleen whales.

鯨魚有著非常進階的聽覺，而且牠們能聽到數公哩遠的聲音。牠們產生低頻率的聲音，能夠探測著廣大的距離。現在許多鯨魚種類都被宣告是瀕臨絕種。除了人類活動，例如違法捕鯨，這些動物可能撞到船或受到漁網纏住。牠們也受到汙染威脅且因氣候改變造成的棲息地損失。現在我將簡短地談論四種類型的鬚鯨。

The first one is the blue whale. The blue whale is the largest animal on the planet. It is also the largest animal ever to have lived, since they are much larger than dinosaurs. Their heart has the same size as a small car, which pumps tons of blood through the circulatory system of the blue whale. The largest blue whale that was ever found was 33.58 meters long and weighed 190 tons. The skin of the blue whale is blue-grey colored. On top of its head, there is a large ridge located from the tip of the nose to the blowhole. The blue whale has a very small dorsal fin and relatively small tail flukes. In terms of feeding and distribution, the blue whale feeds almost exclusively on krill and you can find the blue whales worldwide. They travel to polar waters to feed during summer time and spend the winter in tropical or subtropical oceans. Blue whales like to swim alone or in groups of 2 or 3. In the past century, the blue whale has been extensively hunted and the number has deceased to very low level.

　　第一種是藍鯨。藍鯨是星球上最大的動物。這也是有史以來現存的最大動物，因為牠們比恐龍稍大。牠們的心臟與小型車有著相同的大小，透過藍鯨的循環系統充入數噸的血液。發現的最大的藍鯨是 33.58 公噸長且 190 公噸重。藍鯨的皮膚是藍灰色的。在頭部頂端，有著大型的脊狀隆起，位於噴水孔和鼻子頂端。藍鯨有著非常小的背鰭和相當小的尾部倒鉤。關於攝食和分布，藍鯨幾乎專以磷蝦為食而且你可以在世界各地發現藍鯨的蹤跡。牠們在夏季旅行至極地水域進食，而在冬季於熱帶或亞熱帶現蹤。藍鯨喜歡獨自游泳或以兩人或三人一組的方式游泳。過去這個世紀，藍鯨已經廣泛地受到獵捕且數量已降至非常低的等級。

Hence, it is now listed as an endangered species. The second one I will introduce is the fin whale. The fin whale is a fast swimmer. It can swim at the speed of 30 km/hr. Occasionally, the fin whale would jump out of the water.

The average length of the fin whale is about 18 to 22 meters and it can weigh up to 70 tons. The fin whale looks long and slender, the head resembles the blue whale but the color is dark grey to brown. The fin whale prefers to stay in deep water and it is also distributed all over the world's ocean. Unlike the blue whale, fin whale is more gregarious, which means they live in flocks and are more sociable. Fin whales are generally seen in groups of 10 or more. They mainly feed on small crustaceans, such as crabs, lobsters and shrimps. Northern hemisphere fin whales also feed on fish.

因此，現在被列為瀕臨絕種的物種。第二個我要介紹的是鰭鯨。鰭鯨是快速泳者。牠可以以每小時 30 公里的速度游泳。偶爾，鰭鯨能跳離水中。鰭鯨的平均長度是大概 18 公尺到 22 公尺長而且重達 70 公噸。鰭鯨看起來長且苗條些，頭部與藍鯨相似但是顏色是暗灰到棕色。鰭鯨偏好待在深水水域且也分布至全世界的海洋中。不像藍鯨，鰭鯨較群居性，這意謂著他們成群生活且較社會性。鰭鯨通常以 10 個或更多數量為一組出現在視線中。牠們主要以小型甲殼綱動物，例如螃蟹、龍蝦和蝦子。北半球的鰭鯨也以魚類為食。

The next one is the grey whale, which appears only in the North Pacific Ocean. The grey whale is a baleen whale as well. In summer the grey whales move to the Bering Sea to feed and in winter they travel along the US coast down to the Mexico coast. There are lots of whale watching trips organised and sometimes they swim very close to the whale watching boats. The size of the grey whale is relatively smaller compared with the previous two types. They are 15 meters long on average and weigh about 20 tons. The skin of the back of the grey whale has yellow and white coloured patches caused by parasites. Grey whales are also critically endangered and granted protection from commercial hunting; therefore, they are no longer hunted on a large scale.

下個是灰鯨，牠們僅出現在北太平洋海洋。灰鯨也是鬚鯨的一種。在夏季，灰鯨移至白令海攝食而到了冬季牠們沿著美國海岸旅行至墨西哥海岸。有許多賞鯨旅程的安排而且有時候牠們非常靠近賞鯨船。灰鯨的大小與先前兩種類型相比較小。牠們平均 15 公尺長且大概 20 公噸重。灰鯨背部的皮膚有著由寄生蟲引起的黃色和白色的補塊。灰鯨也出現嚴重性的瀕臨絕種情況，而且授予商業獵捕的保護，因此，牠們也不再受到大規模的獵捕。

The fourth one on our list is the humpback whale. This is probably the most famous whale species because of its songs that could be heard from far distance. Only the male sings. So there is a hypothesis that the humpback whale's song has a reproductive propose. Humpback whales are black all over, and it has a unique way of catching fish, it dives down and circles to the surface. On the way up, fishes are encircled in a bubble net and swallowed by the humpback whale. This type of whale also

影子跟讀「短對話」

影子跟讀「短段落」

影子跟讀「長段落」

travels long distance; they spend winter near Hawaii and move to the polar regions in summer. The humpback whale is up to 19 meters long and 48 tons in weight. It feeds on krill, sardines and small fishes. The humpback whale is considered as a vulnerable species and whaling is prohibited as well.

　　第四種在我們介紹的清單上的是座頭鯨。這可能是最有名的鯨魚種類因為座頭鯨的鳴叫聲能在遠距離就能聽到。僅有雄性座頭鯨鳴叫。所以有個假説是座頭鯨的鳴叫聲有繁殖的目的。座頭鯨全身黑色覆蓋且於捕魚上有獨特的方式。座頭鯨潛入海中並環繞在浮現在水面上。在衝上水面時，魚類環繞在氣泡網中，並且被座頭鯨吞入。這種類型的鯨魚也能夠長距離旅行。牠們冬季會花費時間在夏威夷，而於夏季時移至極地地區。座頭鯨長至 19 公尺長和 48 公噸重。牠以磷蝦、沙丁魚和小型魚類為食。座頭鯨被視為是易受攻擊的物種，而且捕鯨行為也是禁止的。

## ▶▶ 影子跟讀「實戰練習」　🎧 MP3 057

　　此部分為「**影子跟讀實戰練習 ❷**」，請重新播放音檔並完成試題，除了能提升並修正拼寫能力外，也可以藉由音檔注意自己專注力和定位聽力訊息部份，走神或定位錯都會影響在實際考場中的表現，尤其在 section 3 和 4 影響的得分會更明顯，現在就一起動身，開始完成「**實戰練習 ❷**」吧！

There are more than 90 species of whales, all whale species can be categorised into 1.＿＿＿＿＿＿ and toothed whales. The baleen whales eat by swimming slowly through 2.＿＿＿＿＿＿ and straining food into their mouth. And toothed whales as their names indicate, have teeth. Whales live in marine environment and they are mammals. Just like the continental mammals, whales are also 3.＿＿＿＿＿＿, which means they reproduce by giving birth to a calf rather than eggs, which leads to fewer offspring and longer-lived individuals. Whales breathe with their 4.＿＿＿＿＿＿, and they all have 5.＿＿＿＿＿＿ positioned on top of their head. All mammals need to sleep, but whales have to be awake all the time to 6.＿＿＿＿＿＿. So whales have a special sleep 7.＿＿＿＿＿＿.

They produce 8.＿＿＿＿＿＿, which can be detected over large distances. Now many species of whales are declared as endangered. Apart from human activities, such as 9.＿＿＿＿＿＿, these animals could collide with ships or become entangled with 10.＿＿＿＿＿＿. They are also threatened by pollution and 11.＿＿＿＿＿＿ from climate change.

It is also the largest animal ever to have lived, since they are much larger than 12.＿＿＿＿＿＿. Their heart has the same size as a small car, which pumps tons of blood through the 13._____ of the blue whale. The largest blue whale that was ever found was 33.58 meters long and weighed 14._____ tons. The blue whale has a very small 15._____ and relatively small 16._____. In terms of feeding and distribution, the blue whale feeds almost exclusively on 17._____ and you can find the blue whales worldwide.

Hence, it is now listed as an 18._____. The fin whale prefers to stay in deep water and it is also distributed all over the world's ocean. Unlike the blue whale, fin whale is more 19._____, which means they live in flocks and are more sociable. Fin whales are generally seen in groups of 10 or more. They mainly feed on 20._____ such as crabs, lobsters and shrimps.

The next one is the grey whale, which appears only in the North Pacific Ocean. The grey whale is a baleen whale as well. In summer the grey whales move to the 21._____ to feed and in winter they travel along the US coast down to the Mexico coast. They are 15 meters long on average and weigh about 20 tons. The skin of the back of the grey whale has yellow and white 22._____ caused by parasites.

Only the male sings. On the way up, fishes are encircled in a 23._____ and swallowed by the humpback whale. This type of whale also travels long distance; they spend winter near Hawaii and move to the polar regions in summer. The humpback whale is up to 19 meters long and 48 tons weight. It feeds on krill, sardines and small fishes. The humpback whale is considered as a vulnerable species and 24.＿＿＿＿＿＿ is prohibited as well.

## ▶▶ 參考答案

1. baleen whales
2. fish-rich water
3. viviparous
4. lungs
5. blowholes
6. maintain breath
7. pattern
8. low frequency sound
9. illegal whaling
10. fishing nets
11. habitat loss
12. dinosaurs
13. circulatory system
14. 190
15. dorsal fin
16. tail flukes
17. krill
18. endangered species
19. gregarious
20. small crustaceans
21. Bering Sea
22. coloured patches
23. bubble net
24. whaling

# 常考名詞＋生物學專業字 ❷－種內競爭和種間競爭

▶▶ 影子跟讀「實戰練習」 🎧 MP3 058

此篇為**「影子跟讀實戰練習」**，規劃了由聽**「實際考試長度的英文內容」**的 shadowing 練習，提升在考場時的答題**穩定度**和**適應性**，進而獲取理想成績，現在就一起動身，開始聽**「實戰練習」**！

Competition among species or organisms is greater than we can imagine. Resources are finite in a specific region. Competition can occur in plants of the same species competing with each other or plants of different species. Sunlight is the key element for the growth of plants. Plants in tropical rainforests are competing for the same resources, such as sunlight. Some species have evolved to be of such a giant stature that they are able to receive adequate amount of sunlight to survive. Others develop another strategy so that they remain in the understory where light is relatively sparse.

物種或生物有機體間的競爭比我們所能想像的大。資源在特定的地區是有限的。競爭能發生於同物種間的植物彼此競爭或者是發生於不同物種的植物間。陽光是植物生長的關鍵要素。熱帶雨林間的植物彼此間競爭著相同的資源，例如陽光。有些物種已

演化出如此巨大的高度以致於它們能夠接收合宜的陽光而生存。其他植物發展出另一個策略以致於它們維持在陽光相對稀疏的樹林底層。

Apart from sunlight, plants compete for other resources, and intraspecific competition and interspecific competition can occur quite often in regions. The former refers to members of the same species competing for the same resources, and the latter refers to members of distinctive species competing for the same resources. Intraspecific competition can be intense even though members of the same species seem pretty mild with others' presence.

除了陽光，植物競爭著其他資源，而種內競爭和種間競爭能在一個地區頻繁地發生著。前者指的是相同成員的物種競爭著相同的資源，而後者指的是不同成員的物種競爭著相同的資源。種內競爭可以是強烈的，即使相同成員的物種似乎對於其他成員的存在感到相當平和。

Resources are not infinite, so only the most adaptable one can survive. Evolution seems to have a way for species to evolve under the law of the survival of the fittest. Species without a favorable advantage in stature or strength will have a slightest chance to survive since resources are limited. Species not only compete with food resources in specific regions, but also the chances to mate and territory.

資源有限，所以僅有最適應者能夠生存。演化似乎有著一套法則，讓物種遵循著適者生存的法則走。物種沒有在身形或力量上有著最有利的優勢則會有低微的生存機會，因為資源是有限的。物種不僅在特定地區內競爭著食物資源，而且競爭著交配的機會和地域。

In Africa, interspecific competition and intraspecific competition are quite common among the same or different species. The competition among cubs can be seen as the example of the intraspecific competition, whereas the competition among lions and other carnivores can be defined as the example of the interspecific competition. The cubs of the lion are competing with one another for the food captured by female lions. When food resources are abundant, it will not pose any threat to the cubs, but when the food resources are limited, some cubs will die due to a lack of food. The density of the lion populations in a pride of lions also affects the degree of the competition and the survival chance for the cubs.

在非洲，種間競爭和種內競爭在相同物種或不同物種間相當的普遍。幼獸之間的競爭能被視為是種內競爭的例子，而獅子和其他肉食性動物間的競爭則被定義為種間競爭。獅子幼獸們彼此間競爭著由雌性獅子捕獲的食物。當食物資源充分時，對於幼獸們不會造成任何威脅。當時物資源有限時，有些幼獸會因為缺乏

食物而死亡。在獅群中，獅子族群的密度也影響著競爭的程度和幼獸生存的機會。

In addition, interspecific competition and intraspecific competition can occur simultaneously in a specific time-frame. Under the condition where foods are not abundant, interspecific competition can occur among lions and other carnivores, such as cheetahs and hyenas competing for food resources. The intraspecific competition can happen in a pride of lions or prides of lions. Receding water and a change in geography result in competition among prides of lions. They are competing for the territory and foods. Intraspecific competition also occurs in cubs competing for limited foods brought by female lions. Male lions will compete with other male lions which own a pride of lions. They are competing for territories and chances to mate with other female lions. The intraspecific competition can turn the competition into a fierce fight, sometimes between life and death. Male lions which own a pride of lions, if defeated by challengers, will not only lose a pride of lions, but also the life of the cubs. They will be replaced by the challengers. The offspring will be killed by the winners.

此外，種間競爭和種內競爭能在相同的時間框架內發生。在食物不充足的情況下，種間競爭能於獅子和其他肉食性動物間發生，例如獵豹和鬣狗競爭著食物資源。種內競爭能發生在一群獅

子間或獅群和獅群間。水位的退去和地理的改變會導致獅群間的競爭。牠們競爭著領域和食物。種內競爭也能發生在幼獸們競爭著由雌性獅子帶回來有限的食物。雄性獅子會與擁有著其他獅群的雄性獅子們競爭。牠們競爭著領域和與其他雌性獅子交配的機會。種內競爭能轉變成激烈的競爭，有時候是攸關生死的。雄性獅子擁有著獅群。若被挑戰者們打敗，則不僅會失去獅群，也會失去幼獸的生命。雄性獅子會被挑戰者取而代之。後代會被贏家殺死。

There are other cases of competition, too. The inter-specific competition can occur in other forms. Lions, when encountered with greater numbers of hyenas, will ulti-mately have to leave captured foods to them. It may seem unfair from the perspective of humans, but it is for the lives of those lions. Foods can be captured at another time, but harmed bodies will put them in a disadvantaged position in their later lives. Lions, especially female lions, are just relatively larger than hyenas. Surrounded by a group of them can cause a great hazard for the lion, since hyenas are equipped with sharp teeth.

還有其他競爭的例子。種間競爭能以其他形式的方式發生。獅子們，當遭遇較大群的鬣狗時，最終會將捕獲的食物遺留給鬣狗。可能從人類的角度來說似乎不合理，但是卻是為了那些獅子本身的生命。食物可能在其他時間獲取，但受傷的身軀會使牠們在往後的生命中處於不利的位置。獅子，尤其是雌性獅子，僅稍大於鬣狗。當被一群鬣狗圍繞著時，可能會對獅子造成很大的危

險，特別是鬣狗也配有尖銳的牙齒。

Species will evolve to ensure what they do at the moment works best for them. Whether it is the interspecific competition or intraspecific competition, the wheel of evolution will turn organisms or species into the most adaptable form that we see today, and most are endured by the test of time.

物種會演化確保他們在當下做出對於對地們最佳的行為。不論種間競爭或種內競爭，演化之輪將生物有機體或物種轉化成我們現今所看到最適應的模式，而且大多數是受到時間的考驗而存活至今的。

## ▶▶ 影子跟讀「實戰練習」　🎧 MP3 058

此部分為「**影子跟讀實戰練習 ❷**」，請重新播放音檔並完成試題！

Resources are 1.＿＿＿＿＿＿ in a specific region. 2.＿＿＿＿＿＿ is the key element for the growth of plants. Plants in 3.＿＿＿＿＿＿ are competing for the same resources, such as sunlight. Some species have evolved to be of such a 4.＿＿＿＿＿＿ that they are able to receive adequate amount of sunlight to survive. Others develop another strategy so that they remain in the 5._____ where 6._____ is relatively sparse. The former refers to ...... and the latter refers to members of 7._____ species competing for the same resources. Intraspecific competition can be intense even though members of the same species seem pretty 8._____ with others' presence. Resources are not 9._____, so only the most adaptable one can survive. 10._____ seems to have a way for species to evolve under the law of the survival of the fittest. Species without a 11._____ in stature or ...... resources in specific regions, but also the chances to 12._____. The competition among 13._____ can be seen as ...... whereas the competition among 14._____ can be defined as the example of the interspecific competition. The 15._____ of the lion populations .......

In addition, interspecific competition and intraspecific competition can occur simultaneously in a 16._____. Under the condition ...... carnivores, such as 17._____ competing for food resources. Receding 18._____ and a change in 19._____ result in competition among prides of lions. Male lions which own a pride of lions, if defeated by 20._____, will not only lose a pride of lions ...... The 21._____ will be killed by the winners. Lions, when encountered with greater numbers of hyenas, will ultimately have to leave 22._____ to them. Lions, especially 23._____, are just relatively larger than hyenas. Surrounded by a group of them can cause a great 24.＿＿＿＿＿＿＿ for the lion, since hyenas are equipped with sharp teeth. Whether it is the interspecific competition or intraspecific competition, the 25.＿＿＿＿＿＿ ＿＿＿ will turn 26.＿＿＿＿＿＿＿ or species into the most ...... are endured by the test of time.

## ▶▶ 參考答案

| | |
|---|---|
| 1. finite | 2. Sunlight |
| 3. tropical rainforests | 4. giant stature |
| 5. understory | 6. light |
| 7. distinctive | 8. mild |
| 9. infinite | 10. Evolution |
| 11. favorable advantage | 12. mate and territory |
| 13. cubs | 14. lions and other carnivores |
| 15. density | 16. specific timeframe |
| 17. cheetahs and hyenas | 18. water |
| 19. geography | 20. challengers |
| 21. offspring | 22. captured foods |
| 23. female lions | 24. hazard |
| 25. wheel of evolution | 26. organisms |

# 高階名詞❶＋生物學專業字 ❸－動物族群過剩

▶▶ 影子跟讀「實戰練習」　🎧 MP3 059

此篇為「影子跟讀實戰練習」，規劃了由聽「實際考試長度的英文內容」的 shadowing 練習，經由先前的兩個部份的練習，已能逐步掌握聽一定句數的英文內容，現在經由實際考試長度的聽力內容來練習，讓耳朵適應聽這樣長度的英文內容，提升在考場時的答題**穩定度**和**適應性**，進而獲取理想成績，現在就一起動身，開始由聽「**實戰練習**」！（如果聽這部份且跟讀練習的難度還是太高請重複前兩個部份的練習數次後再來做這部分的練習喔！）

With intraspecific competition and interspecific competition, animal populations are regulated within a certain number, but in biology, anything can happen, and there is another phenomenon called animal overpopulation. Explosive growth of a species can lead to the phenomenon of overpopulation. This can occur when a species is introduced in a region where there are no predators. With the absence of the predators, the species can grow uncontrollably. The mechanism of the natural forces loses its ability to control the situation and it will result in ecological imbalance in the region.

隨著種內競爭和種間競爭，動物族群受到規範而維持在特定數量之內，但是在生物學中，任何事都能發生，而且有另一個現象來詮釋，稱作動物族群過剩。物種生長數量暴增能導致族群過剩的現象。這能發生在當一個物種引進至一個地區，而當地沒有掠食者時。因為缺乏掠食者，物種會不受控制地生長著。自然力量的機制失去了控制這個情況的能力，而且它將導致地區內生態不平衡。

If this occurs in the region where there is no human interference, the problem of overpopulation will eventually end when there is depletion of food resources. Without sufficient food resources, the population will experience a dramatic decrease, but when this occurs in places where humans live, additional forces will be added to revert the situation since a non-native species often causes serious problems for the region. Often the solution will be introducing another natural predator of that species to control the overpopulation.

如果發生的是在無人為干擾的地區，族群過剩的問題最終會結束，當食物資源都耗盡時。沒有足夠的食物資源，族群會經歷急遽的下降，但是當情況時發生在人類存活的地區時，額外的力量會來逆轉情勢，因為外來物種通常會對於一個地區造成嚴重的問題。通常解決之道會是引進另一個該物種的天敵來控制族群過剩的問題。

In the history of the animal overpopulation problem,

rabbits when introduced in Australia are one of the mem-orable ones. The rabbit population experienced rapid growth and beyond the control of the local government. Who would have thought that such adorable creatures could cause ecological disturbance and change local peo-ple's perception about rabbits? Rabbits have since then become sinister animals in Australia.

在動物族群過剩的歷史上，兔子，當引進至澳洲時，是其中一個令人記憶深刻的例子。兔子族群經歷急遽的成長而且超過的當地政府的控制。誰能料到如此可愛的生物會導致生態干擾和改變當地人對兔子的看法。兔子自那時候起在澳洲就成為了邪惡的動物。

The story of European rabbits can be traced back to their arrival at the land of paradise, Australia. Without predators, such as foxes and wolves, the breeding led to uncontrollable expansion of rabbits in Australia. The situ-ation went a bit out of control even when natural preda-tors of rabbits were introduced to the region. This puzzled people who deemed it would be a perfect solution for controlling the population at that time. Australian animals were faced with intense intraspecific competition with rabbits since they were relatively mild. The inability to compete with the so-called invasive species, the Europe-an rabbits would lead to a decline in other species and make this method useless since foxes were more inclined to eat sluggish Australian animals. Eventually, most Australian animals experienced starvation, and the ecological loss was unimaginable and unbearable for Australia.

歐洲兔子的故事能追溯至牠們來到天堂樂土，澳洲。沒有掠食者，例如狐狸和狼，在澳洲繁殖導致無法控制兔子擴大生殖的局面。情勢有點超過控制，即使當兔子的天敵引進至該地區時。這也使得人們感到困惑，因為他們認為這會是當時控制族群數量的完美解決辦法。澳洲動物面臨著與兔子間激烈的種內競爭。澳洲動物相對地溫和，無能力與所謂的外來物種匹敵，歐洲兔子會導致其他物種的下降而這也使得這個方法無效，因為狐狸更傾向食用懶散的澳洲動物。最終，大多數澳洲動物經歷了飢餓，而且生態損失對澳洲來說是難以想像且難以忍受的。

Rabbits might possess certain traits that make them so powerful in Australia, but no one holds all the cards. A lot of methods have been used to control the situation. Ultimately, biocontrol seemed to be the most plausible one. The Myxoma virus is the virus only fatal to European rabbits not American rabbits, and the virus has the selectivity so that it is totally harmless to local farm animals and humans. The Australian government used the virus and successfully controlled the increasingly rampant rabbit population.

兔子可能擁有使牠們能在澳洲如此強大的特徵，但是沒人總是佔盡優勢。有許多方法已經用於控制這個情況。最終，生物控

制似乎是最合理的解決方式。黏液瘤病毒，一種僅對於歐洲兔子致命但對美國兔子則否的病毒，此病毒有選擇性所以對於當地的農場動物和人類全然無害。澳洲政府使用此病毒且成功地控制了日益猖獗的兔子族群。

This can be a great case for people learning this phenomenon. Anything greater than normal can create problems. In nature, every species exists for a specific reason. Species are regulated under the law of the survival of the fittest. Species all have a specific and unique function in the food web. No species should be overprotected. Any imbalance will cause unimaginable ecological loss and sometimes it is not something we can dial back. The story of European rabbits can be reversed back to the controllable situation by using the virus, but we cannot be certain what is going to happen in other situations where problems of animal overpopulation or non-native species introduced in the region will be solved. No one can guarantee things will be easily solved, and no one can guarantee current technology or any method will work out or what may happen.

　　這對於學習此現象的人們來說可以是很棒的案例。任何事情超過正常標準都會造成問題。在自然界中，每個物種存在都有特定的理由。物種在適者生存的法則下受到規範。物種在食物鏈中總有特定和獨特的功能。沒有物種應該被過度保護。任何失衡都能導致無法想像的生態損失，而且有時候不是我們能將局面撥回

正軌的。歐洲兔子的故事可以藉由病毒而逆轉回受控制的局面，但是，在確定動物族群過剩或外來種引進到一個地區的問題受到解決時，我們無法確切知道接下來會發生的其他情況。沒有人可以保證事情會輕易的解決，而且沒人可以保證現今科技或任何方法會對於可能發生的問題有效。

## ▶▶▶ 影子跟讀「實戰練習」 🎧 MP3 059

　　此部分為**「影子跟讀實戰練習 ❷」**，請重新播放音檔並完成試題，除了能提升並修正拼寫能力外，也可以藉由音檔注意自己專注力和定位聽力訊息部份，走神或定位錯都會影響在實際考場中的表現，尤其在 section 3 和 4 影響的得分會更明顯，現在就一起動身，開始完成**「實戰練習 ❷」**吧！

　　With intraspecific competition and interspecific competition, animal populations are 1.＿＿＿＿＿＿＿ within a certain number, but in 2.＿＿＿＿＿＿, anything can happen, and there is another phenomenon called 3.＿＿＿＿＿＿. This can occur when a species is 4.＿＿＿＿＿＿ in a region where there are no predators. It will result in 5.＿＿＿＿＿＿ in the region.

　　If this occurs in the region where there is no 6.＿＿＿＿＿＿, the problem of overpopulation will eventually end when there is 7.＿＿＿＿＿＿ of food resources. Without sufficient food resources, ...... since a 8._____ often causes serious problems for the region. Often the solution will be introducing another 9._____ of that species to control the overpopulation.

In the history of the animal overpopulation problem, 10._____ when introduced in Australia ...... cause 11._____ and change local people's perception about rabbits? Rabbits have since then become 12._____ in Australia.

The story of European rabbits can be traced back to their arrival at the land of paradise, 13._____. Without predators, such as 14._____, the breeding led to ...... compete with the so-called 15._____, the European rabbits ...... make this method useless since foxes were more inclined to eat 16._____.

The Myxoma virus is the virus only 17._____ to European rabbits not American rabbits, and the virus has the 18._____ so that it is totally harmless to 19._____ and humans. The Australian 20._____ used the virus and successfully controlled the increasingly rampant rabbit population.

In nature, every species exists for a specific reason. Species are regulated under the law of the 21._____.

Species all have a specific and unique function in the food web. Any imbalance will cause unimaginable 22._____ and sometimes it is not something we can dial back. The story of European rabbits can be reversed back to the 23._____ by using the virus, but ...... and no one can guarantee 24._____ or any method will work out or what may happen.

## ▶▶ 參考答案

1. regulated
2. biology
3. animal overpopulation
4. introduced
5. ecological imbalance
6. human interference
7. depletion
8. non-native species
9. natural predator
10. rabbits
11. ecological disturbance
12. sinister animals
13. Australia
14. foxes and wolves
15. invasive species
16. sluggish Australian animals
17. fatal
18. selectivity
19. local farm animals
20. government
21. survival of the fittest
22. ecological loss
23. controllable situation
24. current technology

# 高階名詞❷＋生物學專業字❹－剋星

▶▶ 影子跟讀「實戰練習」 🎧 MP3 060

　　此篇為「**影子跟讀實戰練習**」，規劃了由聽「**實際考試長度的英文內容**」的 shadowing 練習，經由先前的兩個部份的練習，已能逐步掌握聽一定句數的英文內容，現在經由實際考試長度的聽力內容來練習，讓耳朵適應聽這樣長度的英文內容，提升在考場時的答題**穩定度**和**適應性**，進而獲取理想成績，現在就一起動身，開始由聽「**實戰練習**」！（如果聽這部份且跟讀練習的難度還是太高請重複前兩個部份的練習數次後再來做這部分的練習喔！）

　　In *Return of the Condor Heroes*, the successful portrayal of bees and spiders at the cave incident inadvertently solves the problem for the characters trapped in the cave. In the scene, Chou Bao Tung was at first lured by Zhao Zhi Jing to a cave and bitten by an extremely poisonous spider, known as the spider with five colorful colors. The spider of this kind can be quite deadly and no one could find a cure at that time. The villains are so confident of the fatal venom produced by the spider that they think Chou Bao Tung is doomed, but what they fail to take into account is how another character, Xiaolongnu knows about the basis of biology. Species, though powerful, all have their natural enemies. The solution she comes up with is quite a clever one. From Chou's expressions that venom of bees somehow eases the pain of spider bite, she figures out the nemesis of the spider could be bees. She uses a swarm of bees to fly into the exceedingly large spider web, and then the venom of the bees can dilute the spider venom in Chou's body. The venom of bees can act as an antidote to the spider bite.

在《神鵰俠侶》中，洞穴事件中成功描繪了蜜蜂和蜘蛛不經意地替受困於洞穴中的角色解決問題。在場景中，周伯通首先被趙志敬誘至洞穴，且被極毒的毒蜘蛛，名為五彩雪蜘蛛所咬傷。這個種類的毒蜘蛛可以致命而且在當下無人能解。惡棍因此對於由蜘蛛產的的致命毒液相當有自信，認為周伯通完蛋了，但是他們沒有考慮到的是其他角色，小龍女了解生物學的基本原理。物種，儘管強大，都有著牠們的天敵。她所想到的解決之道是相當聰明的。從蜜蜂毒液某種程度地減輕他被蜘蛛咬的痛楚的表情中，她找到了蜘蛛的剋星可能是蜜蜂。她使用一群蜜蜂衝破了極大張的蜘蛛網，然後用蜜蜂的毒液稀釋周體內的蜘蛛毒。蜜蜂的毒液可以充當成蜘蛛咬傷的解藥。

The story of *Return of the Condor Heroes* provides a glimpse into the natural world. The plot of bees being rescuers is very successful. It turned a deadlocked situation into one with a silver lining. In the natural world, the fight of creatures often amazes us, and the rule is always the same. Natural enemies exist somewhere else with the amazing creatures we know. In some forests, we are able to witness the victory of tarantulas, whether it is the ambush to capture creatures like some insects or whether it is the killing of the larger creatures like snakes. We are astonished by how the poisonous fangs and venom they inject into the victim's body, but we are also able to see how these seemingly powerful creatures encounter the bitter fight with their natural enemies. Tarantulas can be the target of wasps and become paralyzed by the sting of the wasp. The chance of the escape is almost none since the wasp can even repeatedly sting the tarantulas. What is more horrific is that spiders are not dead right on the spot. They are just temporarily paralyzed. The neurotoxic venom makes the victim a zombie. The victim will be offered to the wasp's offspring. This is a cruel treatment that a natural enemy does to its prey.

　　神鵰俠侶的故事提供了自然世界的一瞥。使用蜜蜂當作拯救者的情節很成功。它將僵局轉變成希望之光。在自然界中，生物間的戰鬥常使我們感到驚艷，而且規則總是千篇一律。天敵存在於我們所知道的驚人生物的某處。在有些樹林間，我們能夠目睹狼蛛的勝利，不論是狼蛛的埋伏以捕捉像是有些昆蟲或是殺死像是蛇那樣較大的生物，但是我們也能夠看到那些看似強大的生物面對著天敵時所陷入的苦戰。狼蛛可以是黃蜂的目標而且會因為黃蜂的螫咬而癱瘓。逃脫的機會渺茫，因為黃蜂甚至可以重複性的叮咬狼蛛。更令人感到可怕的是，蜘蛛並不會於當場斃命。牠們僅是暫時性地癱瘓。神經毒素使得受害者成了殭屍。受害者將

會被提供給黃蜂的後代食用。這是天敵對於牠們的獵物來說所做出的殘酷對待。

In addition to the remarkable ability of wasps, the close relative of the wasp, hornets, are also fascinating. They are able to take down larger insects, such as mantises, which provide their offspring with a large source of protein. They contain larger venom than typical wasps. They are considered as quite incredibly cruel predators since hornets stage a large battle to other bee colonies, carrying with them the larvae and adults for their young. The massacre can destroy an entire bee colony. It is not an individual fight like what a wasp does to a tarantula. The fight involves hundreds of corpses. It is the example of the cannibalization about what hornets can not only do to other insects but the species of the similar kind, such as honey bees.

除了黃蜂卓越的能力之外，黃蜂的近親，大黃蜂也是吸引人的。大黃蜂能夠打倒體型較大的昆蟲，例如螳螂，以提供牠們後代大量的蛋白質。比起黃蜂，牠們包含較大量的毒液。牠們也被視為是相當驚人地殘酷掠食者，因為黃蜂可以策劃與其它蜂群的大型戰鬥，將牠們的幼蟲和成年蜂提供給大黃蜂幼蟲食用。此屠殺可以毀掉整個蜂群。這不只是個人戰鬥，像黃蜂對於狼蛛那般。戰鬥牽涉到幾百個屍體。這是同類相殘的例子，一個關於大黃蜂不僅能對於其他昆蟲，而且對相似物種，例如蜜蜂所做的行為。

The relationship between bees and spiders, hornets

and bees help us understand the wonder of the natural world. The cure of certain bites from some creatures can be found in other species. Although wasps prevail in the fight with insects and spiders, there are bee-eaters and other natural enemies of wasps out there waiting for the meal. Bees can be cannibalized by similar but larger species of their kind, such as hornets. Whether it is the relationships between different species or similar species, nature has its own mechanism to regulate the population. The fate of tarantulas or a colony of bees is not something for us to decide. It's evolved under the law of the survival of the fittest and sometimes reasons behind these are unexplained and mysterious.

蜜蜂和蜘蛛的關係、大黃蜂和蜜蜂的關係幫助我們了解了大自然的驚奇。由某些生物特定的咬傷的解藥可能於其他物種中發現。儘管黃蜂在與昆蟲和蜘蛛的戰鬥中獲取勝利，還是有食蜂鳥和其他黃蜂的天敵存在，等著享用黃蜂大餐。蜜蜂可以被相似但較於牠們本身大的物種同類相殘，例如大黃蜂。不論在不同物種或相同物種間的關係，自然有著規範族群的機制。狼珠的命運或一群蜜蜂的命運不是由我們來決定的。這是經由適者生存的法則下演化，而且有時候背後的理由是無法解釋且神祕的。

## ▶▶ 影子跟讀「實戰練習」 🎧 MP3 060

此部分為「**影子跟讀實戰練習 ❷**」，請重新播放音檔並完成試

題，除了能提升並修正拼寫能力外，也可以藉由音檔注意自己專注力和定位聽力訊息部份，走神或定位錯都會影響在實際考場中的表現，尤其在 section 3 和 4 影響的得分會更明顯，現在就一起動身，開始完成「**實戰練習 ❷**」吧！

In *Return of the Condor Heroes*, the successful 1._____ _____ of bees and spiders at the cave incident inadvertently solves the problem for the characters trapped in the 2.\_\_\_\_ _____. The spider of this kind can be quite 3._____ \_\_\_\_ and no one could find a cure at that time. The 4._____ _____ are so confident of the 5._____ produced by the spider that they think Chou Bao Tung is doomed, but what they fail to take into account is how another character, Xiaolongnu knows about the basis of 6._____. Species, though powerful, all have their natural enemies. The solution she comes up with is quite a clever one. From Chou's expressions that venom of bees somehow eases the pain of the 7._____, she figures out the 8._____ \_\_\_\_ of the spider could be bees. She uses a swarm of bees to fly into the exceedingly large 9._____, and then the venom of the bees can 10._____ the spider venom in Chou's body. The venom of bees can act as an 11.\_\_\_\_ _____ to spider bite.

Natural enemies exist somewhere else with the 12.\_\_\_\_ _____ we know. In some forests, we are able to witness the victory of 13._____, whether it is the ambush to capture creatures like 14._____ or whether it is the killing of the larger creatures like snakes. We are astonished by how the poisonous fangs and venom they inject into the victim's body, but we are also able to see how these seemingly powerful creatures encounter the bitter fight with their natural enemies. The chance of the escape is almost none since the 15._____ can even repeatedly sting the tarantulas. What is more horrific is that spiders are not dead right on the spot. They are just 16._____. The neurotoxic venom makes the victim a 17._____. The victim will be offered to the wasp's offspring. This is a 18._____ _____ that a natural enemy does to its prey.

In addition to the remarkable ability of wasps, the close relative of the wasp, 19._____, are also fascinating. They are able to take down larger insects, such as 20._____ _____, which provide their offspring with a large source of 21._____. They contain larger venom than typical wasps. They are considered as quite incredibly cruel predators since hornets stage a large battle to other 22._____ \_\_\_\_, carrying with them the 23._____ and adults for their young. The 24._____ can destroy an entire bee colony. It is not an individual fight like what a wasp does to a tarantula. The fight involves hundreds of 25._____. It is the example of the 26._____ about what hornets can not only do to other insects but the species of the similar kind, such as honey bees.

Bees can be 27.＿＿＿＿＿＿＿ by similar but larger species of their kind, such as hornets. It's evolved under the law of the survival of the fittest and sometimes reasons behind these are 28.＿＿＿＿＿＿＿.

## ▶▶ 參考答案

| | |
|---|---|
| 1. portrayal | 2. cave |
| 3. deadly | 4. villains |
| 5. fatal venom | 6. biology |
| 7. spider bite | 8. nemesis |
| 9. spider web | 10. dilute |
| 11. antidote | 12. amazing creatures |
| 13. tarantulas | 14. some insects |
| 15. wasp | 16. temporarily paralyzed |
| 17. zombie | 18. cruel treatment |
| 19. hornets | 20. mantises |
| 21. protein | 22. bee colonies |
| 23. larvae | 24. massacre |
| 25. corpses | 26. cannibalization |
| 27. cannibalized | 28. unexplained and mysterious |

影子跟讀「短對話」

影子跟讀「短段落」

影子跟讀「長段落」

# 國家名＋月份＋生物學專業字 ❺－母性本能和對子女的養育

▶▶ 影子跟讀「實戰練習」　🎧 MP3 061

　　此篇為「**影子跟讀實戰練習**」，規劃了由聽「**實際考試長度的英文內容**」的 shadowing 練習，經由先前的兩個部份的練習，已能逐步掌握聽一定句數的英文內容，現在經由實際考試長度的聽力內容來練習，讓耳朵適應聽這樣長度的英文內容，提升在考場時的答題**穩定度**和**適應性**，進而獲取理想成績，現在就一起動身，開始由聽「**實戰練習**」！（如果聽這部份且跟讀練習的難度還是太高請重複前兩個部份的練習數次後再來做這部分的練習喔！）

　　Maternal instinct has been known about for a long time. The definition of it is the inclination that a mother will do to protect her young, and it is believed that the ability is innate and is wired into the brain. Parenting, on the other hand, involves parents' way of raising and educating their kids. Both are quite essential for the development and growth of the youth. Infants have too little control of outer forces and have little knowledge of how to react to a certain situation. Sometimes we find it hilarious that parents or mothers in the animal kingdom resemble parents or human being mothers so much. Some use a loose approach by leaving their kids out there. Others have such an extensive care for their kids that it astonishes most of us.

　　母性本能長久以來一直為人所知。母性本能的定義是母親會為自己的小孩所做出保護的傾向，而且據說這個能力與生俱來且連接到腦部。對子女的養育，另一方面，則包含了父母的養育方式和教育小孩的方式。兩者對於幼年小孩的成長和發展都相當重要。嬰兒對於外在的力量有很少的控制能力且沒有足夠的知識去應對特定的情況。有時候我們覺得動物世界中的父母或雌性很滑稽，因為牠們與人類的父母或母親相似。有些使用了較鬆散的方式，放任小孩子在那裡。其他父母則對於小孩有著極大的照護而使我們大多數人感到驚奇。

　　In Africa, for example, carnivores roam on the savanna and sometimes cubs after being born have little protection from their moms. Other times, it is because parents are starting to learn how to be one. It is not some innate skill. Take lions, for example, older ones are professional and experienced. They know how to hide the cubs from other predators, such as hyenas and cheetahs. They cover up the smell of the cubs so that predators will not find them. Younger lions are less experienced, and a lousy one can sometimes find its young not in the place she hides them. The likelihood of the young getting eaten by other predators is exceedingly high especially after searching for a long time.

影子跟讀「短對話」

影子跟讀「短段落」

影子跟讀「長段落」

例如，在非洲，肉食性動物漫遊在草原上，因為有時候幼獸們在出生後從母親身上得到少少的保護。其他時候，因為父母才開始學習如何當個父母。這不是一些與生俱來的技能。以獅子為例，年長的獅子們是專業且有經驗的。他們知道如何將幼獸藏起，免於其他掠食者，例如鬣狗和獵豹的侵擾。牠們覆蓋了幼獸的氣味所以其他掠食者找不到牠們。較年輕的獅子們較不具經驗，而且糟糕者可能有時候會發現幼獸不在牠所藏匿的地點裡了。幼獸被其他掠食者捕食的可能性極高，特別是在找尋很久都無所獲後。

　　In the lion world, some mothers exhibit greater strength than other mothers in the pride. Raising the cub without the protection of a pride of lions, is pretty much like a single mom raising kids without a father in the human world. It is an admirable trait that people find it commendable. Pressure is high for individual female lions living without a pride, especially having a cub to raise and worry about. Food captured by female lions can be stolen by nosy and opportunistic animals, such as hyenas. A well-structured lion system can successfully guard cubs from the danger of carnivores and prevent things such as food from being stolen.

　　在獅子的世界裡，有些雌性展現比群體中的雌性較大的力量。養育著無獅群保護的幼獸是相當類似於在人類世界中，一位單親母親養育小孩卻沒有父親一樣。這是令人欽佩的特質，而人們認為是讚譽可嘉的。對沒有獅群的個體雌性獅子來說，壓力是

很大的，特別是有個幼獸要養育和擔心。由雌性獅子所捕獲的食物可能被煩人且機會主義的動物，例如鬣狗奪走。結構完整的獅群系統就能夠成功地保衛幼獸們免於受到肉食性動物的危險和像是使食物免於被偷的情形發生。

In India, it is a whole different world. Female sloth bears show strong maternal instinct for the young. Infant bears on the back of the mother bears are the common scene. They are well-protected by their mother. During the 9 month period, the enjoyment of being on the back of their mother makes them the enviable creatures of other creatures which do not show such extensive care. During the time of living with their mom, infant sloth bears are capable of learning lots of things from their mothers, such as skills to hunt and the ability to find foods.

在印度，卻又是另一個全然不同的世界。雌性懶熊對於幼子展現出強烈的母性本能。幼兒熊待在母親的背上是常見的場景。牠們受到牠們母親的妥善的保護。在九個月大的時期，牠們待在母親背上所得到的享受使牠們成為受人稱羨的生物，對照著其他對於幼子沒有展現出極大照護的動物。在與母親居住的期間，幼兒懶熊也能從牠們的母親身上學習到許多事情，像是捕獵和尋找食物的能力。

The major threat for sloth bears comes from tigers. Tigers sometimes hunt sloth bears for food. Often tigers will not attack mother sloth bears with cubs since maternal instinct will make them ruthlessly fight back and tigers will not gain anything from the attack. On rare occasions, they mess with mother sloth bears, and mother sloth bears exhibit the fight-to-death mode, aggressively attacking the tiger. It demonstrates the Chinese saying that being a mother makes you stronger than you think.

對懶熊來説，最主要的威脅來自於老虎。老虎有時候會補獵懶熊做為食物。通常老虎不會攻擊攜帶著幼獸的懶熊母親，因為母性本能會讓牠們無情的還擊，而且老虎不會從攻擊中獲取任何好處。在罕見的情況下，老虎打擾到母親懶熊，母親懶熊展現了戰到死的模式，侵略性地攻擊老虎。這顯示了中國俗諺説的身為母親使你比想像中更強大。

While a sloth mother shows the well-protected care for their young, cuckoos adopt a leisurely approach, similar to what some people do in the human world leaving kids for others to take care of. In the human world, we have babysitters. In the eastern world, there are grandparents who are willing to do the job for you. Cuckoos use a clever way to get the other birds to raise their babies. They are sneaky and irresponsible parents deceiving other birds into being a free babysitter till their kids are full-grown. As humans, we all question and condemn this kind of behavior even if the behavior has been evolving for quite a long time. Deep in our hearts, no one wants to raise a kid to 18 years old and later find out the kid is not yours. It's just parenting in an odd way, I think.

　　當懶熊母親對於他們的幼子展現了完整的保護，杜鵑鳥卻採取休閒式的方針，類似於人類世界中有些人將小孩放給其他人照顧一樣。在人類世界中，我們有褓母。在東方世界，有祖父母非常願意要替你照顧小孩。杜鵑鳥使用了聰明的方式讓其他鳥來養育幼子。牠們是卑鄙且不負責任的父母，欺騙其他鳥類去充當免費的小孩褓母直到牠們的小孩長大。作為人類，我們都質疑且譴責這樣的行為，即使這樣的行為已經演化了相當長的一段時間。在我們內心深處，沒有人想要養育小孩到 18 歲大然後卻於之後發現小孩並非你親身的。我想，這只是養育小孩的奇怪方式吧。

## ▶▶ 影子跟讀「實戰練習」　🎧 MP3 061

　　此部分為**「影子跟讀實戰練習 ❷」**，請重新播放音檔並完成試題，除了能提升並修正拼寫能力外，也可以藉由音檔注意自己專注力和定位聽力訊息部份，走神或定位錯都會影響在實際考場中的表現，尤其在 section 3 和 4 影響的得分會更明顯，現在就一起動身，開始完成**「實戰練習 ❷」**吧！

　　1.＿＿＿＿＿＿ has been known about for a long time. The definition of it is the 2.＿＿＿＿＿＿ that a mother will do to protect her young, and it is believed that the ability is innate and is wired into the 3.＿＿＿＿＿＿. 4.＿＿＿＿＿＿ have too little control of outer forces and have little 5.＿＿＿＿＿＿ of how to react to a certain situation. Some use a 6._____ by leaving their kids out there. Others have such an 7._____ for their kids that it astonishes most of us.

In 8._____, for example, 9._____ roam on the 10._____ and sometimes cubs after being born have little protection from their moms. They know how to hide the cubs from other predators, such as 11._____. They cover up 12._____ of the cubs so that predators will not find them. The 13._____ of the young getting eaten by other predators is exceedingly high especially after searching for a long time. Raising the cub without the 14._____ of a pride of lions, is pretty much like a single mom raising kids without 15._____ in the human world. 16._____ is high for 17._____ living without a pride, especially having a cub to raise and worry about. Foods captured by female lions can be stolen by nosy and 18._____, such as hyenas.

In 19._____, it is a whole different world. 20._____ show strong maternal instinct for the young. They are well-protected by their mother. During the 21._____ period, the 22._____ of being on the back ...... of other creatures which do not show such extensive care. On rare occasions, they mess with mother sloth bears, and mother sloth bears exhibit the fight-to-death 23._____, aggressively attacking the tiger.

While a sloth mother shows the well-protected care for their young, 24.＿＿＿＿＿＿＿＿ adopt a leisurely approach, similar to what some people do in the human world leaving kids for others to take care of. In the human world, we have 25.＿＿＿＿＿＿＿. They are sneaky and irresponsible parents deceiving other birds into being the free babysitters till their kids are 26.＿＿＿＿＿＿.

## ▶▶ 參考答案

| | |
|---|---|
| 1. Maternal instinct | 2. inclination |
| 3. brain | 4. Infants |
| 5. knowledge | 6. loose approach |
| 7. extensive care | 8. Africa |
| 9. carnivores | 10. savanna |
| 11. hyenas and cheetahs | 12. the smell |
| 13. likelihood | 14. protection |
| 15. a father | 16. Pressure |
| 17. individual female lions | 18. opportunistic animals |
| 19. India | 20. Female sloth bears |
| 21. 9 month | 22. enjoyment |
| 23. mode | 24. cuckoos |
| 25. babysitters | 26. full-grown |

影子跟讀「短對話」

影子跟讀「短段落」

影子跟讀「長段落」

# 數字＋常見名詞＋商學專業字 ❶－心理學：咖啡和複利效應

▶▶ 影子跟讀「實戰練習」　🎧 MP3 062

　　此篇為「影子跟讀實戰練習」，規劃了由聽「實際考試長度的英文內容」的 shadowing 練習，經由先前的兩個部份的練習，已能逐步掌握聽一定句數的英文內容，現在經由實際考試長度的聽力內容來練習，讓耳朵適應聽這樣長度的英文內容，提升在考場時的答題穩定度和適應性，進而獲取理想成績，現在就一起動身，開始由聽「實戰練習」！（如果聽這部份且跟讀練習的難度還是太高請重複前兩個部份的練習數次後再來做這部分的練習喔！）

　　A cup of coffee from big brands? Hmm... so tempting. Sorry for setting a bad example myself, but it's actually a good start for today's topic "the compound effect". What does a cup of coffee have to do with this? Everyday whether you are on your way to the office, or whether you are feeling exhausted after a long day at school, it's so tempting to have a cup of coffee, sitting in a comfy chair and a room with a perfect lighting. All of a sudden, fatigue and other things are overridden...like it's just a cup of coffee or it's just NT150 dollars.

　　一杯來自咖啡大廠的咖啡…嗯…如此吸引人…抱歉自己做了

很不好的示範，但是實際上卻是今天主題「複利效應」很好的開端。一杯咖啡與這個有甚麼關聯性呢？每天不論你是前往上班途中或是你在學校漫長的一天後身感疲憊，有杯咖啡是如此吸引人，坐在舒適的椅子和有著恰如其分的燈光下。突然間，疲累和其他事情都被蓋過了…像是只是一杯咖啡或者是僅花費 150 元新台幣。

Although we have been warned or urged not to spend money buying a coffee, we just cannot help buying it whenever we feel there is a need for us to lighten up our mood or something. We have put behind what many experts have said or mentioned in those articles. But little things do matter. Doing a basic calculation yourself, you can surely find how significant that is. Accumulated fees can somehow astound most of us.

雖然我們已受到警告或規勸不要將金錢花費在購買咖啡，但是每當我們覺得有需要能讓我們打起精神或什麼的，我們又無法克制地買了它。我們將許多專家所說的話或在那些文章中提到的部分都拋諸到腦後。但是這一丁點的小事卻至關重要。自己做一個基本計算，你可以確定發現影響會是多麼重大。累積的費用令我們大多數的人感到吃驚。

Let me do a basic calculation for you. A white-collar office lady who buys another brand's coffee, whose price is significantly lower than that of the big brand's. Say 55 NT dollars for a latte. She buys a cup of coffee per day.

There are 52 weeks in a year. She buys 5 cups of coffee per week. We multiply that by 52, and the result is NT14300 dollars per year.

讓我做簡單的計算給你們看。一個白領上班族女性買了其他品牌的咖啡，價格遠比大廠牌的咖啡便宜。假定是每杯拿鐵 55 元新台幣的價格。她每天都買一杯咖啡。一年裡頭共有 52 週。她每週買 5 杯咖啡。我們將每杯價格乘以 52，結果是每年將花費新台幣 14300 元。

## | Student A |

Wow...that certainly is significant to today's salary. No wonder, an expert once said, if you're earning a 22k salary right after you graduate, then you probably shouldn't be drinking coffee of huge brands, and it's the accumulated fee of other brands...Coffee of other brands is almost one thirds of huge brand's coffee, and I'm not drinking it even if I'm earning more than a 22k salary.

## | 學生 A |

哇…這對於現今的薪水真的很可觀。難怪有專家曾說，如果你是畢業後賺取 2 萬 2 千元月薪的人，那麼你可能真的不該喝大廠牌咖啡。這是其他品牌的累加費用…其它廠牌的咖啡花費幾乎是大廠牌咖啡的三分之一，即使我的薪水高於 22K 我也不喝它。

## | Professor |

That's pretty smart.

| 教授 |

相當聰明。

## Student A

Sometimes people just don't think it's a big deal or something. That's why people have a hard time looking at what's in their pocket at the end of the month. They have no idea where they've spent the money and they don't seem to recall what they have spent it on. It's a small thing that we can easily ignore. According to the fee calculation, you can buy an iPhone, if you quit drinking coffee for two years.

| 學生 A |

有時候人們不認為這是什麼大事或什麼的。這也是為什麼人們在每個月月底的期間，看著他們的荷包面有難色。他們不知道自己將金錢花費到哪裡了和他們回憶不起他們將錢花費在什麼上面了。這是很些微的小事，而我們卻輕易地忽略。根據累加的費用，你可以購買一隻 iPhone 了，如果你停止飲用咖啡兩年。

## Professor

Excellent observations. Now I want to show you a basic calculation. NT 150 dollars per cup, 5 cups per week, 52 weeks per year. We are looking at NT39000 dollars which is close to two months' income for a new grad. It's scary. We are responsible for every choice we make. Every day we tend to ignore little things. Some of my stu-

影子跟讀「短對話」

影子跟讀「短段落」

影子跟讀「長段落」

dents even have loans, but they are not making smart choices. They live paycheck to paycheck, not realizing it is the little things they have to pay attention to. So, I want you all to start your day by being acutely aware of the decisions you make.

卓越的觀察。現在我想要藉基本的計算。每杯咖啡是新台幣 150 元，一週五杯，一年 52 周。我們在看台幣 39000 元。幾乎是一個畢業生近兩個月的月薪。這相當驚人。我們必須對於我們每個選擇負起責任。每天我們傾向忽略相當微不足道的小事情。我的學生中有些人甚至有學生貸款，他們每天卻沒有做出每個聰明的選擇。他們是月光族，沒有意識到是這些小事情才是他們需要注意的部分。所以我想要你們在每一天都很清楚自己所做的決定。

Being willing to change is always a great start in life. For example, before starting a family of my own, I used to buy unnecessary things, thinking that money is easily earned. Now I don't want to drink coffee any more. Instead I drink water. A lot of water per day. Imagine how much money I have saved for the past two decades. The saved money can be used for other purposes, too. Another thing which also relates to today's topic "the compound effect" is the calorie. You're not only saving money, but calories.

願意改變總是生活中很棒的開始。例如，在我自己成家前，

我過去曾購買許多不必要的東西，認為金錢是很容易賺取的。現在我不在喝咖啡了。取而代之的是我喝水，每天大量的水。想像在過去這 20 年中，我省了多少錢。節省的金錢也能夠用於其他用途上。另一件關於今天主題「複利效應」的是卡路里。你能節省不僅是金錢，還有卡路里。

You can do a basic calculation youself...I'm not doing it for you. You can check the beverage you frequently drink, and do a basic calculation. You'll also be astonished by the calories you have consumed over the year. You get to utilize the theory in so many ways and your life will improve significantly...Look at me...a slim figure at my age. I'm saying NO to desserts that go well with coffee, but I do enjoy watching my colleagues do so. Just kidding! Now please open to page 52..it's a theory that is related to what we've discussed so far......

你可以自己替自己計算一下…我沒有要替你們計算。你可以檢查每個你常喝的飲料，做下基本的計算。你會發現過去一年裡你攝取了多少卡路里且感到吃驚。你能夠在很多地方使用這個理論，而且你的生活會有顯著的改變…看我…以我的年紀來說，我是苗條的。我也拒絕品嚐與咖啡極搭的甜點，但是我很享受看著我的同事去做這件事…沒有啦…只是開玩笑！現在請翻開到第 52 頁…是關於一個我們目前為止所討論過的理論…。

　　此部分為「**影子跟讀實戰練習 ❷**」，請重新播放音檔並完成試題，除了能提升並修正拼寫能力外，也可以藉由音檔注意自己專注力和定位聽力訊息部份，走神或定位錯都會影響在實際考場中的表現，尤其在 section 3 和 4 影響的得分會更明顯，現在就一起動身，開始完成「**實戰練習 ❷**」吧！

　　Sorry for setting a bad example myself, but it's actually a good start for today's topic "the 1.＿＿＿＿＿＿＿". Everyday whether you are on your way to the 2.＿＿＿＿＿＿＿, or whether you are feeling exhausted after a long day at school, it's so tempting to have a cup of coffee, sitting in a 3.＿＿＿＿＿＿＿ and a room with a perfect lighting. All of a sudden, 4.＿＿＿＿＿＿＿ and other things are overridden... like it's just a cup of coffee or it's just NT5.＿＿＿＿＿＿＿.

　　We have put behind what many 6.＿＿＿＿＿＿＿ have said or mentioned in those articles. But little things do matter. Doing a basic 7.＿＿＿＿＿＿＿ yourself, you can surely find how significant that is. Accumulated 8.＿＿＿＿＿＿＿ can somehow astound most of us.

　　A white-collar 9.＿＿＿＿＿＿＿ who buys another brand's coffee, whose price is significantly lower than that of the big brand's. Say 55 NT dollars for a 10.＿＿＿＿＿＿＿. She buys a cup of coffee per day. There are 11.＿＿＿＿＿＿＿

__ in a year. She buys 5 cups of coffee per week. We multiply that by 52, and the result is NT 12._____ per year.

No wonder, an expert once said, if you're earning a 13._____ right after you graduate, then you probably shouldn't be drinking coffee of huge brands, and it's the accumulated fee of other brands...

Sometimes people just don't think it's a big deal or something. That's why people have a hard time looking at what's in their 14._____ at the end of the month. According to the fee calculation, you can buy an 15._____, if you quit drinking coffee for two years.

We are looking at NT 16._____ which is close to two months' income for a new grad. It's scary. We are responsible for every choice we make. Every day we tend to ignore little things. Some of my 17._____ even have 18._____, but they are not making smart choices.

Being willing to change is always a great start in life. For example, before starting a 19._____ of my own, I used to buy unnecessary things, thinking that 20._____ is easily earned. Now I don't want to drink coffee any more. Instead I drink water. Another thing which also relates to today's topic "the compound effect" is the calorie. You're not only saving money, but 21._____ .

You can do a basic calculation youself...I'm not doing it for you. You can check the 22._____ you frequently drink, and do a basic calculation. You get to utilize the 23.__ _____ in so many ways and your life will improve significantly...Look at me...a 24._____ at my age. I'm saying NO to 25._____ that go well with coffee, but I do enjoy watching my colleagues do so. Just kidding! Now please open to 26._____ .

## ▶▶ 參考答案

| | |
|---|---|
| 1. compound effect | 2. office |
| 3. comfy chair | 4. fatigue |
| 5. 150 dollars | 6. experts |
| 7. calculation | 8. fees |
| 9. office lady | 10. latte |
| 11. 52 weeks | 12. 14300 dollars |
| 13. 22k salary | 14. pocket |
| 15. iPhone | 16. 39000 dollars |
| 17. students | 18. loans |
| 19. family | 20. money |
| 21. calories | 22. beverage |
| 23. theory | 24. slim figure |
| 25. desserts | 26. page 52 |

影子跟讀「短對話」

影子跟讀「短段落」

影子跟讀「長段落」

# 高階名詞❸＋生物學專業字 ❻－生物學：共同演化，蟆螈和束帶蛇

▶▶ 影子跟讀「實戰練習」　🎧 MP3 063

　　此篇為「**影子跟讀實戰練習**」，規劃了由聽「**實際考試長度的英文內容**」的 shadowing 練習，經由先前的兩個部份的練習，已能逐步掌握聽一定句數的英文內容，現在經由實際考試長度的聽力內容來練習，讓耳朵適應聽這樣長度的英文內容，提升在考場時的答題**穩定度**和**適應性**，進而獲取理想成績，現在就一起動身，開始由聽「**實戰練習**」！（如果聽這部份且跟讀練習的難度還是太高請重複前兩個部份的練習數次後再來做這部分的練習喔！）

## | Professor |

I promise I won't bore you with The Origin of XXX...(chuckling) ...actually it's not that boring...I'm beginning today's session by telling you today's topic...it's not that remote as it seems...It's very close to us actually. Today's topic is co-evolution. Co is a prefix which means together. Co-evolution means species evolving together...

## | 教授 |

　　我保證我不會用「**XXX 的起源**」這本書來讓你們感到無聊透頂…（笑）…實際上它沒那麼無聊…我會告訴你們今天的課程來作為開頭…它不會像看起來那麼遙不可及…它與我們實際上息息

相關。今天的主題是共同演化。CO 字首意謂著「一起」的意思。共同演化意謂著物種一起的演化。

Let's take a look at the definition. "In biology, coevolution occurs when two or more species reciprocally affect each other's evolution", and it includes different forms, such as mutual relationships, host-parasite, and predator-prey. This somehow fascinates me...Like how can they benefit or influence other organisms? Growing up on a farm, I can almost taste the nature of all forms, capturing moments that snakes chasing their prey, witnessing their fangs injecting venom in the prey.

我們來看一下定義。「在生物學裡，共同演化發生於兩個或多個物種相互影響著彼此的演化」。共同演化包括不同的形式，像是相互關係、宿主和寄生關係和捕食者和獵物間的關係。這也或多或少令我感到沉迷。像是他們如何受益於或影響其他的生物有機體。於農場中長大，我可以幾乎嚐到大自然的各種形式，捕捉到蛇追捕他們獵物的時刻，目睹他們毒牙注射毒液到獵物裡。

But biology seems to have a way of its own. There are all kinds of mechanisms out there. Sometimes prey have developed a certain defense mechanism to protect themselves from danger. For example, chameleons camouflage themselves. A great deception to natural predators. Even if the camouflage doesn't work out sometimes, this reduces their chances of getting captured by predators. The successful survival rate is increasing for the species. Other times, you can spot species exhibiting all forms of colors, but they are doing this not because they want to allure the mate, like peacocks showing their feathers. They are doing this because colorful colors tell predators that probably they have venom and they are not as pleasant as they seem.

　　但是生物學似乎有著自己的機制。有許多種的機制。有時候獵物發展出特定的防禦機制來保護自己免於危險。例如，變色龍偽裝自己。對自然界中的捕食者是最大的欺騙。即使偽裝有時候沒有發揮作用，這降低了他們被捕食者捕抓的機會。對物種來說生存成功率增加了。其他時候，你可以察覺到物種展示出所有形式的顏色，但是他們這麼做並不是他們想要吸引伴侶，像是孔雀展示自己的羽毛那樣。他們這麼做是因為多彩的顏色能夠告訴捕食者，可能他們有毒而且他們沒有看起來那樣美味。

## | Student A |

　　Yep...I once saw golden dart frogs with different kinds of colors. They're pleasing to the eye. I like the blue one. Their venom is incredibly poisonous. Snakes that accidentally eat them can die in a second. It's pretty scary. They have colors that say "don't touch me". Some chameleons use color changes to scare away their predators, too. Although sometimes they still get eaten by some snakes. Sometimes they are like decorations in the rainforest. Their venom is used for different purposes. For example, the toxin is used on arrows for hunting. But what does this have to do with coevolution?

## | 學生 A |

　　是的⋯有次我看到有著各種不同顏色的箭毒蛙。很滿足視覺觀感。我喜歡藍色的。他們的毒性非常強。蛇不經意吃到箭毒蛙會一下子就死亡。這相當驚人。牠們有顯示著「別碰我」的顏色。有些變色龍也使用顏色變化嚇走捕食者，儘管有時候變色龍仍被有些蛇類捕食。有時候牠們像是雨林裡的裝飾品。牠們的毒性已經被利用於不同的地方，例如，毒性置於箭上頭用來捕獵。但是這與共同演化有什麼關聯性呢？

## | Professor |

I'm about to tell you. Don't be so hasty. here're other animals that use coloration to advertise their toxicity, too. For example, salamanders have vivid colors to ward off predators. They secrete neurotoxins, too. Neurotoxins on their skin can be a powerful weapon to protect them. A big bullfrog accidentally eating a salamander can eventually open its mouth and set the salamander free. Predators like snakes will eventually avoid animals with cryptic colors, such as salamanders and golden dart frogs, but the fact is they all have their natural enemies, too.

## | 教授 |

　　我正要告訴你們⋯別這麼急嘛⋯有其他動物也會使用顏色宣傳著它們的毒性。例如，蠑螈有著鮮豔的顏色抵禦捕食者。牠們

也分泌神經毒素。牠們皮膚上的神經毒素是保護它們的強大武器。大型的牛蛙不經意吃到蠑螈最終會將嘴巴張開並釋放蠑螈。捕食者像是蛇最終會避開捕食具神秘顏色的動物，像是蠑螈和箭毒蛙，但是事實是牠們也都有自己的天敵。

Garter snakes, also known as ribbon snakes, are the predator of salamanders simply because they are not afraid of the toxin contained in the salamander's bodies. When you see a snake, which does not hesitate to attack salamanders, you're probably seeing a garter snake. They're just having their own snack time.

襪帶蛇也以束帶蛇而為人所知是蠑螈的捕食者，僅因為牠們不懼怕蠑螈身體內所含的毒素。當你看到蛇毫不猶豫地攻擊蠑螈…你可能看到襪帶蛇。那是牠們的零食時間。

They have developed a mechanism to resist the neurotoxins of the salamanders. This is a pretty remarkable improvement for biology. Ribbon snakes are undergoing a series of mutations to evolve a mechanism so that they are unafraid of the neurotoxins. Salamanders, on the other hand, are gradually evolving to a more powerful toxin to counter ribbon snakes' development. Surprisingly, garter snakes are continually evolving a stronger mechanism. This is what we call coevolution. This is the perfect example of the prey-and-predatory coevolution. It's like a race. Amazing, right? Salamanders and ribbon snakes are constantly seeking for ways to improve their way in order to survive. I just don't want you to feel bad for those salamanders. It's just part of the process of the natural selection.

牠們已經發展出抵抗蠑螈的神經毒素。這是生物學中相當驚人的進步。束帶蛇正經歷一系列的突變演化出機制，如此牠們就不懼怕神經毒素。蠑螈，另一方面，也逐漸演化出更強大的毒素來反制束帶蛇的進展。驚人地是，襪帶蛇正持續演化出更強的機制。這就是我們所稱的共同演化。這是獵物和捕食者共同演化的絕佳例子。這像是場比賽。令人吃驚，對吧？蠑螈和束帶蛇不斷地尋找方式來改進自我才得以生存。我不會希望你們對於那些被捕食的蠑螈感到難過。這只是天擇的一部分過程。

## | Student A |

That's pretty amazing. Are we going to see the videos or will we be introduced to another form of coevolution today?

## | 學生 A |

這相當驚人，我們會觀看視頻或我們今天會介紹另一個形式的共同演化嘛？

## | Professor |

I guess we'll do that in the next session. Now, I want to tell you more about ribbon snakes. They are venomous, and like salamanders, they secrete neurotoxins, too.

The venom they produce is pretty mild compared with that of other snakes, such as rattle snakes and cobras.

│教授│

我想我們會在下堂課討論。現在我想要告訴你們更多關於束帶蛇的部分。牠們實際上有毒，就如同蠑螈那樣，牠們也分泌神經毒素。只是相較於響尾蛇與眼鏡蛇等其他蛇類，牠們所分泌的神經毒素溫和許多。

## ▶▶▶ 影子跟讀「實戰練習」　🎧 MP3 063

此部分為「**影子跟讀實戰練習 ❷**」，請重新播放音檔並完成試題，除了能提升並修正拼寫能力外，也可以藉由音檔注意自己專注力和定位聽力訊息部份，走神或定位錯都會影響在實際考場中的表現，尤其在 section 3 和 4 影響的得分會更明顯，現在就一起動身，開始完成「**實戰練習 ❷**」吧！

Co is a 1.＿＿＿＿＿＿ which means together. Co-evolution means species evolving together...

Let's take a look at the 2.＿＿＿＿＿＿. "In biology, 3.＿＿＿＿＿＿ occurs when two or more species reciprocally affect each other's evolution", and it includes different forms, such as mutual relationships, 4.＿＿＿＿＿＿, and predator-prey. Growing up on 5.＿＿＿＿＿＿, I can almost taste the nature of all forms, capturing moments that 6.＿＿＿

_____ chasing their prey, witnessing their fangs injecting venom in the prey.

There are all kinds of 7._____ out there. For example, 8._____ camouflage themselves. A great 9._____ to natural predators. Even if the camouflage doesn't work out sometimes, this reduces their chances of getting captured by predators. The successful 10._____ rate is increasing for the species. Other times, you can spot species exhibiting all forms of colors, but they are doing this not because they want to allure the mate, like 11._____ showing their 12._____. They are doing this because colorful colors tell predators that probably they have venom and they are not as 13._____ as they seem.

Yep...I once saw golden dart frogs with different kinds of colors. They're pleasing to the eye. I like the 14._____ one. Their venom is incredibly 15._____. Snakes that accidentally eat them can die in a second.

It's pretty awesome to see golden dart frogs. They are like decorations in the 16._____. Their venom is used for different purposes. For example, the toxin is used on 17._____ for hunting. But what does this have to do with coevolution?

I'm about to tell you. Don't be so hasty. here're other animals that use coloration to advertise their 18._____, too. For example, 19._____ have vivid colors to ward off predators. A big 20._____ accidentally eating a salamander can eventually open its mouth and set the salamander free. Predators like snakes will eventually avoid animals with cryptic colors, such as salamanders and golden dart frogs, but the fact is they all have their natural enemies, too.

Garter snakes, also known as 21._____, are the predator of salamanders simply because they are not afraid of the toxin contained in the salamander's bodies. They're just having their own 22._____ time.

This is a pretty remarkable improvement for biology. Ribbon snakes are undergoing a series of 23._____ to evolve a mechanism so that they are unafraid of the neurotoxins. Salamanders, on the other hand, are gradually evolving to a more powerful 24._____ to counter ribbon snakes' development. Surprisingly, garter snakes are continually evolving a stronger mechanism Salamanders and ribbon snakes are constantly seeking for ways to improve their way in order to survive. It's just part of the process of the 25._____.

The venom they produce is pretty mild compared with that of other snakes, such as rattle snakes and 26._____.

## ▶▶ 參考答案

| | |
|---|---|
| 1. prefix | 2. definition |
| 3. coevolution | 4. host-parasite |
| 5. a farm | 6. snakes |
| 7. mechanisms | 8. chameleons |
| 9. deception | 10. survival |
| 11. peacocks | 12. feathers |
| 13. pleasant | 14. blue |
| 15. poisonous | 16. rainforest |
| 17. arrows | 18. toxicity |
| 19. salamanders | 20. bullfrog |
| 21. ribbon snakes | 22. snack |
| 23. mutations | 24. toxin |
| 25. natural selection | 26. cobras |

# 高階名詞＋生物學專業字 ❼－海洋生物學：探討甲殼綱、鯨類和鰭足類動物

▶▶ 影子跟讀「實戰練習」　🎧 MP3 064

此篇為「影子跟讀實戰練習」，規劃了由聽「**實際考試長度的英文內容**」的 shadowing 練習，經由先前的兩個部份的練習，已能逐步掌握聽一定句數的英文內容，現在經由實際考試長度的聽力內容來練習，讓耳朵適應聽這樣長度的英文內容，提升在考場時的答題**穩定度**和**適應性**，進而獲取理想成績，現在就一起動身，開始由聽「**實戰練習**」！（如果聽這部份且跟讀練習的難度還是太高請重複前兩個部份的練習數次後再來做這部分的練習喔！）

## | Professor |

As you can see from the video, a crab stays pretty vigilant on the shore. All of a sudden, an octopus shows up unannounced dragging the crab, which struggles hard to escape, into the water. This demonstrates octopus' another victory on land. Octopuses have been known for their high intelligence, remarkable camouflage, and ink. They are the master of the marine creatures. Their inborn talent allows them to inhabit different marine habitats.

從視頻中你可以看到，螃蟹在岸上保持高度警戒。然後突然間，章魚無聲地出現，把仍在掙扎的螃蟹拖進水裡。這顯示了章

魚在陸地上的另一個勝利。章魚以牠們高度的智力、驚人的偽裝和墨水聞名。牠們是海洋生物中的主宅者。章魚天生的能力顯示出它們居住於不同的海洋棲地。

Crustaceans and mollusks are on their food list. Prey will be injected with a paralyzing saliva and disjointed with their beaks. Clams and crabs, although equipped with a hard shell, can't withstand the toxic saliva they secrete. The enzyme of the saliva will dissolve the calcium structure of the shell. Without the protection of the shell, the prey will be consumed in an instant.

甲殼綱動物和軟體動物都在牠們的食物清單上。獵物會被注射具癱瘓能力的唾液並會被章魚的喙肢解。蛤蠣和螃蟹，儘管都裝備著堅硬的外殼，卻無法抵禦章魚分泌的唾液毒素。唾液中的酵素會將鈣結構的殼分解。沒有了外殼的保護，獵物就會即刻被食用。

Even though they seem powerful compared to some fish, crustaceans, and mollusks, octopuses have their natural enemies, too. They can be preyed on by cetaceans, sharks, pinnipeds, sea otters, or sea birds, but recently, an astounding video revealed a giant octopus taking down a shark, too...perhaps they're not that approachable and meek, right? They can be as aggressive as they seem.

即使牠們在有些魚、甲殼綱動物和軟體動物中看似強大，章

魚也有牠們自己的天敵。牠們會被鯨類動物、鯊魚、鰭足類動物、海獺或海鳥捕食，但最近一個驚人的視頻揭露大型章魚也拿下鯊魚…或許牠們沒那麼容易接近或溫和，對吧？牠們跟看起來一樣具攻擊性。

## | Student B |

It's incredible...I'm still having a hard time believing that. The video captures the phenomenal attack of the octopus. Poor shark...but it somehow shows that size matters when it comes to an attack...like small snakes getting eaten by a larger lizard and a full-grown mantis can take down a very small snake...

## | 學生 B |

這很難以置信…仍需要些時間來消化這個事實。視頻捕捉到非凡的章魚攻擊畫面。可憐的鯊魚。但某種程度上來說，這顯示出當提到攻擊時，這跟體態有關。像是小型蛇被較大的蜥蜴捕食，體態生長成熟的螳螂能夠拿下體態非常小的蛇一樣。

## | Professor |

That's correct. We can't really tell who's winning until It's near the end... A doomed prey can sometimes find itself a moment to escape...All of a sudden it totally saves itself from being the meal of another creature. Or a predator can successfully plot the whole scheme to capture its prey in a moment. All prey have their defense mechanisms, too.

| 教授 |

正確。不到最後我們無法得知誰是贏家。劫數難逃的獵物可能有時候發現了能逃走的時刻。突然間，它救了自己免於成為其他生物的餐點。或者是捕食者能成功的密謀計劃整個騙局於片刻間捕到獵物。所有個獵物也都有它們的防禦機制。

| Professor |

Oops! ...totally forgot to mention the definition of them. Crustaceans may seem like a big word but they are often the food we order when we're in a restaurant. I think you know what they are. For example, shrimps, crabs, and lobsters belong to the category of the crustaceans. We eat them very often. Like octopuses, we have to break down their harden armor to eat the soft tissue inside. Cetaceans, on the other hand, are much bigger than crustaceans. They are familiar to us as crustaceans. Let me list three cetaceans for you...or is there anyone else who wants to try that...

| 教授 |

喔～都忘了要提關於牠們的定義。甲殼綱動物似乎像個大詞彙，但牠們通常就是我們在餐廳時會點的食物。我認為你知道牠們為何？蝦子、螃蟹和龍蝦都屬於甲殼綱動物的範疇。我們很常以牠們為食。至於章魚，我們必須要拆解牠們堅硬的裝甲來吃裡頭柔軟的組織。鯨類動物，另一方面，是比甲殼綱動物更大的生物。牠們也同甲殼綱動物為我們所熟悉。讓我列出三個鯨類動物給你。或者是有任何人想要試試看。

## | Student B |

Whales...dolphins...and porpoises...

## | 學生 B |

鯨魚⋯海豚⋯和鼠海豚。

## | Professor |

Excellent! Let's continue...pinnipeds are another word for seals. They are semi-aquatic marine mammals...pinnipeds, cetaceans, and crustaceans are all familiar marine mammals to us...Let's go back to what we've discussed. The defense mechanism. Octopuses have their own defense mechanisms, too. They secrete ink. They are equipped with an ink sac, so when threatened, they spew out an ink cloud to distract their predator⋯so that they will have a higher chance to escape. The vision of the predators is blocked by a sudden pouring of the ink. This will give octopuses a few seconds to escape. Sometimes they are lucky enough to escape...at other times...it just won't work.

## | 教授 |

優秀⋯讓我們繼續⋯鰭足類動物是海豹的換句話說。牠們是半水生海洋哺乳類動物。鰭足類動物、鯨類動物和甲殼綱動物都是我們所熟悉的海洋哺乳類動物。讓我們回到我們已經討論過的部分，防禦機制。章魚也有自我的防禦機制。牠們分泌墨水。牠們配有墨水囊，所以當受到威脅時，牠們會噴出墨水雲來分散捕

食者的注意…如此一來就有更多的逃生機會。捕食者的勢力會受到突然湧現的墨水阻擋。這會給章魚幾秒時間逃生。有時牠們能很幸運的逃走，但有時這並不管用。

Aside from the ink cloud, octopuses are venomous. Blue-ringed octopuses are extremely venomous. In nature, having venom gives you an upper hand. It more or less protects you from getting eaten, unless the predator is immune to the potency of the venom or the predator coevolves to be resistant to the venom. Also, the coloration also exhibits as a warning to the predator. It sends out a clear message, "Don't come near me!"

除了墨水雲之外，章魚也有毒性。藍環章魚異常的毒。在自然界中，有毒性讓你佔上風。這或多或少能保護你免於被捕食，除非捕食者能免於毒性的效力或捕食者共同演化出對毒性的抵抗力。而且，顏色也顯示出對捕食者的警告。毒性傳遞出清楚的訊息：『別靠近我！』

With summer vacation coming up... as a professor, I've got to warn you about jellyfish and blue-ringed octopuses. They sometimes surface to a shallow water. Blue-ringed octopuses are especially deadly to humans. So just be careful when you swim in the shallow water. When threatened, they are not lovely and docile as they seem. The toxicity of the blue-ringed octopuses can kill you in a minute. I guess that's all for today.

影子跟讀「短對話」　影子跟讀「短段落」　影子跟讀「長段落」

隨著暑假的到來，身為教授，我想要提醒你們關於水母和藍環章魚。牠們有時候會浮現到淺水水域。藍環章魚對人類有致命的傷害。所以當你游泳在淺水水域時要小心。當受到威脅時，藍環章魚不會像看起來的那樣可愛且溫馴。藍環章魚的毒性能於片刻間殺了你。我想今天就到這邊。

## ▶▶▶ 影子跟讀「實戰練習」 🎧 MP3 064

此部分為**「影子跟讀實戰練習 ❷」**，請重新播放音檔並完成試題，除了能提升並修正拼寫能力外，也可以藉由音檔注意自己專注力和定位聽力訊息部份，走神或定位錯都會影響在實際考場中的表現，尤其在 section 3 和 4 影響的得分會更明顯，現在就一起動身，開始完成**「實戰練習 ❷」**吧！

As you can see from the video, a 1._____ stays pretty 2._____ on the shore. All of a sudden, an octopus shows up unannounced dragging the crab, which struggles hard to escape, into the water. This demonstrates octopus' another 3._____ on land. Octopuses have been known for their high intelligence, remarkable 4._____, and ink. They are the master of the marine creatures. Their inborn talent allows them to inhabit different 5._____.

Crustaceans and 6._____ are on their food list.

Prey will be injected with a paralyzing 7._____ and disjointed with their beaks. Clams and crabs, although equipped with a 8._____, can't withstand the toxic saliva they secrete. The 9._____ of the saliva will dissolve the 10._____ structure of the shell.

They can be preyed on by cetaceans, 11._____, pinnipeds, 12._____, or sea birds, but recently, an astounding video revealed a giant octopus taking down a shark, too....

Poor shark...but it somehow shows that size matters when it comes to an attack...like small snakes getting eaten by a 13._____ and a full-grown mantis can take down a very small snake...All of a sudden it totally saves itself from being the meal of another creature. Or a predator can successfully plot the whole scheme to capture its prey in a moment. All prey have their 14._____ mechanisms, too.

Crustaceans may seem like a big word but they are often the food we order when we're in a 15._____. I think you know what they are. For example, 16._____, crabs, and 17._____ belong to the category of the crustaceans. We eat them very often.

Yes, marine creatures...marine mammals...to be more

影子跟讀「短對話」

影子跟讀「短段落」

影子跟讀「長段落」

specific...they are welcomed 18._____ like we often see them perform in the 19._____ or circus...

Excellent! Let's continue...pinnipeds are another word for 20._____. They are semi-aquatic marine mammals...pinnipeds, cetaceans, and crustaceans are all familiar marine mammals to us... They secrete ink. They are equipped with an 21._____, so when threatened, they spew out an ink cloud to distract their predator... so that they will have a higher chance to escape. The 22._____ of the predators is blocked by a sudden pouring of the ink.

Aside from the ink cloud, octopuses are 23._____. In nature, having venom gives you an upper hand. It more or less protects you from getting eaten, unless the predator is immune to the potency of the venom or the predator coevolves to be resistant to the venom. Also, the 24._____ also exhibits as a warning to the predator. It sends out a clear message, "Don't come near me!" With 25._____ coming up... as a professor, I've got to warn you about 26._____ and blue-ringed octopuses. They sometimes surface to a shallow water. Blue-ringed octopuses are especially deadly to humans.

## ▶▶ 參考答案

| | |
|---|---|
| 1. crab | 2. vigilant |
| 3. victory | 4. camouflage |
| 5. marine habitats | 6. mollusks |
| 7. saliva | 8. hard shell |
| 9. enzyme | 10. calcium |
| 11. sharks | 12. sea otters |
| 13. larger lizard | 14. defense |
| 15. restaurant | 16. shrimps |
| 17. lobsters | 18. mammals |
| 19. zoo | 20. seals |
| 21. ink sac | 22. vision |
| 23. venomous | 24. coloration |
| 25. summer vacation | 26. jellyfish |

影子跟讀「短對話」

影子跟讀「短段落」

影子跟讀「長段落」

國家圖書館出版品預行編目(CIP)資料

一次就考到雅思聽力7⁺ / Amanda Chou著.
-- 初版. -- 新北市：倍斯特, 2019.08面；
公分. --（考用英語系列；19）
ISBN 978-986-97075-9-6（平裝附光碟）
1.國際英語語文測試系統　2.考試指南

805.189　　　　　　　　　　　108011584

考用英語系列　019

# 一次就考到雅思聽力7⁺（附英式發音MP3）

初　　版　　2019年8月
定　　價　　新台幣460元

作　　者　　Amanda Chou
出　　版　　倍斯特出版事業有限公司
發 行 人　　周瑞德
電　　話　　886-2-8245-6905
傳　　真　　886-2-2245-6398
地　　址　　23558 新北市中和區立業路83巷7號4樓
E-mail　　best.books.service@gmail.com
官　　網　　www.bestbookstw.com
總 編 輯　　齊心瑀
企劃編輯　　陳韋佑
封面構成　　高鍾琪
內頁構成　　菩薩蠻數位文化有限公司
印　　製　　大亞彩色印刷製版股份有限公司

港澳地區總經銷　　泛華發行代理有限公司
地　　址　　香港新界將軍澳工業邨駿昌街7號2樓
電　　話　　852-2798-2323
傳　　真　　852-3181-3973